Downing Dominic

Cliff J. Cavender

Cavender Books

Contents

Dedication

To all those who struggle to let themselves be happy

Chapter 1

Aaron Watkins

THIS CANCER CONFERENCE MAY be the most pivotal experience of my career.

Scratch that—the most pivotal experience *of my life*. Because if I don't find someone to fund my research here, I can kiss my brief stint as an assistant professor goodbye. And that means no way to research the cure for leukemia, the disease that took my little sister's life, broke up my family with steep medical bills, and led me to endure a childhood marred by neglect.

I step out from my Uber and walk to the doors of the massive Marriott Conference Center, my carry-on rolling on the sidewalk a steady scraping sound against the din that is New York City. I'm dressed in a blue button-down and black slacks, which feel tighter than I remember. Six months ago, I started lifting again, so I assume this feeling is because of muscle gain. At least I hope so. People say they see a difference in me, but all I can sense is a greater appetite.

Focus, Aaron.

I take a deep breath and loosen a notch on my belt, already feeling the relief. On this trip, I promised myself I wouldn't worry about how I look. I have a much more important task to focus on. Besides, body dysmorphia to gay men has always been a persistent wraith, stalking us and waiting until we're most vulnerable to strike. In therapy, I've learned it's best not to pay these poor thoughts about my body any mind, especially when I'm anxious. Instead, I try to remind myself that I'm a beefy, hairy guy, and that all my meat sits in just the right places. Plus, it's not like I'm looking to impress a potential partner. Or even casually fuck. My entire focus is on my research and how to eliminate the scourge of leukemia. I don't have time for anything or anyone else.

In the hotel lobby, I pass by some of the wealthiest people that the United States has to offer, all dressed in outfits obviously crisper than mine. I have to take another deep breath to keep my heartrate from speeding out of control.

Just one person, I remind myself. *I just need to find one person willing to fund my leukemia research.*

Overwhelmed by the bustling crowd, I step to a lonely part of the hotel lobby. I sit down on my carry-on and pull out my phone to read a text I just got, my thick thighs threatening to tear my tight pants at their seams.

"My ride's almost there," my friend Laura says. "I'll see you soon." I reply with a thumbs-up emoji, then mindlessly scroll through Instagram to calm myself as I wait for her.

The anticipation of seeing my best friend from grad school puts me slightly at ease. We both came into our cancer biology program as bright-eyed undergraduates, blissfully unaware of the trials we were about to experience. Grad school was the crucible that forged our platinum-strength bond. We've remained close since, even after her marriage and us taking jobs at different universities. Even her being seven months pregnant hasn't stopped our weekly phone call check-ins and daily exchange of memes. This woman has been a mainstay in my life for nearly six years.

Thank God we're sharing a room this weekend—she's always helped me maintain a level head, and Lord knows I need it if I'm going to convince some millionaire to personally fund me. If my goddamned mentor hadn't embezzled all that money, then maybe I wouldn't be in this position. But it is what it is. It's Thursday night, and I have the next three days to find just one person. I try to tell myself that there's plenty of time, but my racing heart makes me feel otherwise.

On Instagram, I come across an ad about the college football team at Miss U, my alma mater in Mississippi, and immediately refresh my feed so it goes away. Overall, I got a good education there, but seeing anything about their football team brings up bad memories. Specifically, bad memories about a very handsome man who went off to play for the NFO. One who played as a legendary defensive tackle for Miss U but insisted I take his virginity. One who I could have called my boyfriend if he didn't need to keep his sexuality a secret. One who, to my chagrin, sneaks into my brain every time I'm even remotely horny. And sometimes, when I catch my mind drifting, I just wish I could hear his voice again.

With him on my mind, I open up my notes app without thinking. There I find the several drafts of unwritten texts and emails that I never sent him. Apologies, in essence. Part of me wonders if I could have undid the hurt I caused by sending them.

Then I close the notes app with a sigh and just stare at nothing. I eliminated such thinking long ago. Even if I could undo what I did, the relationship would have found some other way to end. It was inevitable. He was to be a closeted man in the NFO, so a gay relationship could never work. Part of me worries I'll see him here, but I don't need to worry about that.

I've heard of some big football players—Kyle Weaver, for example—coming to these events to look for organizations to donate to. Apparently, like me, he's also lost a loved one to cancer. But my old flame? Chances of him doing this are slim to none. Football is all he cares about. He has that as his career, and I have mine as a cancer researcher, which leaves me no time to date, anyways. There's no way we'll ever cross paths again.

"Aaron!" a familiar voice calls out.

My head shoots up, happy to be distracted from the memory of ex-almost-boyfriend, and I see a very pregnant Laura rushing toward me. She's wearing a tasteful sundress, and her curly black hair bounces as she jogs.

I stand up to greet her, and she inserts herself in my open arms. I try my best not to put too much pressure on her stomach.

"So good to see you," I say over her shoulder.

She pulls away and strikes a flamboyant pose. "It's good to see me, isn't it?"

I roll my eyes and laugh. She's been re-obsessed with *Wicked* ever since the new movie came out.

When we met in our first-year seminar, we discovered that we both adore musicals. I can confidently say that watching them with her is what got me through that grueling first year alone. When I've told other masculine gay men my obsession for musicals, some have balked, wondering how some tall, bearded, and broad man can like something so feminine. And that's when I usually tell them, sometimes in nicer words or sometimes verbatim, to fuck off.

"Are you doing good?" she asks. "Ready to find someone to fund your research?"

I put my hands on my hips and let out a sigh, the deepest one I've released all day.

"Oh my god," she says. "Your shoulders—you've gotten so big."

I release my arms from my hips and fold them, blushing. "Oh, stop it," I say. "And yeah, I'm as ready as I'll ever be."

She shakes her head. "I still can't believe that a professor at Admiral University—one of the best universities in the Midwest—was caught embezzling university funds."

"Yeah," I say with a sharp exhale through my nose. "The funds I thought were going to keep my research afloat until I got tenure."

She puts her hands on my shoulders. "You got this. I believe in you. Use my belief in you so you can have your own," she says, alluding to "Just One Person" from the *Snoopy* musical, which she always brings up when I need encouragement. "You'll find someone to fund you."

"Thank you," I say, squeezing her hands. "How are you..." But I drift off when I realize that she's got none of her luggage with her.

"Your bags," I say, panicking. "Did you forget them in your Uber or something?"

She looks at me confused, and that's when I see her husband Patrick walking through the Marriott doors with two carry-ons.

"Patrick," I say as he walks up to us. "A pleasant surprise. Didn't know you were joining us this weekend."

"Good to see you too," he says, but he's as puzzled as Laura. "Did she not tell you?"

And then a look of pure horror spreads across Laura's face. "Oh my God. I forgot."

My stomach sinks. "Tell me what?" I ask. Ever since I received that call from our chair about my mentor and his felony, I haven't reacted well to surprises.

She slams her palm against her forehead, leaving a red mark. "This damn pregnancy brain."

Patrick starts rubbing her back as she pinches the bridge of her nose, her eyes shut in frustration.

"Patrick and I got a hotel farther away," she says. "With my pregnancy, we didn't know when we'd get the chance to vacation out of Minnesota for a while. So we wanted to do some touristy things while we were here."

My chest tightens a bit, sad that I won't be rooming and catching up with my best friend. "Okay, that makes sense," I say. "What about our room?"

"I called and told them to consolidate the room into a one bed so it wouldn't be as expensive," she says. "But it's our treat. I paid for it." She shakes her head. "I thought I told you all this, but everything's been a fog."

"Wow, you didn't need to pay for all of it," I say.

"It's our pleasure," Patrick says. "We're sorry to inconvenience you."

"You both have nothing to worry about," I say. "I totally understand."

"Are you sure?" Laura asks. "If you need, you can stay with us."

I shake my head. "No. You guys deserve this vacation time together. Besides, I need as much time here so I can talk to more people. Commuting here would just take the time away from finding funding."

She sighs. "Thanks for understanding. I really came here to meet with a colleague and see you. We'll spend more time in between some sessions."

"Of course. It's no worries," I say. I'm disappointed, but at least I still have my room. Plus, I want to be as accommodating as possible to Laura right now. This is her first time being pregnant, after all.

"We should probably go meet with your colleague," Patrick says. "We have that dinner reservation in an hour."

"Right," Laura says. "Thanks for the reminder. I clearly need it."

"I'll check into my room," I say. "But I'll see you tomorrow?"

She nods. "At the opening session? Absolutely."

We hug goodbye, and then I make my way to the long line that is the hotel check-in. I run my hand through my thick black hair, blowing a sigh out of my pursed lips.

This is fine. Not ideal, but manageable. If I get too overwhelmed and Laura's not around, I can call her, or I can message my therapist. This will be good. I'll be fine.

As I step forward in line, I notice the ass of the man standing in front of me. Because it's perfect, the kind that could make any mildly attractive man look hot as hell. I've always been an ass man. But as I take in the man's entire body, I realize that this is the body of one of the most attractive men I've ever seen. And that's not because I can see his face—I can't. He's facing away from me. It's because I recognize who he is.

My old flame from Miss U.

The man whose virginity I took.

The man I've never been able to stop thinking about, even after all these years.

Dominic Johnson.

The line ahead of him moves up, and I robotically step forward, my panic causing my brain and body to separate for just a moment. But Dominic doesn't lift his head. So he doesn't see the line move. So I barrel right into his back, the top of my crotch perfectly pressing against his plump ass.

He stumbles and apologizes, which he doesn't need to do because it wasn't his fault. But that's when he looks back at me, and my entire body goes cold. He looks me in the eye, then does a double take. Then, he fully faces me, his entire body tense with anger, and I know it's not because I just ran into him.

It's because of how I left him seven years ago.

The line moves up again, but he doesn't budge. His fists tighten, and his jaws clench as he glares at me.

"Hey, Dominic," I say. "Long time no see."

Chapter 2

Dominic Johnson

I STAND IN LINE to check-in to my room at the hotel, tapping my foot on the carpet when I'm not moving forward.

This plan better work. I mean, it works for Kyle Weaver, so why not me? I move forward a place in line, and I feel slightly better about it.

If I find a reputable organization or research project at this cancer conference to fund, I can get good press coverage about it just like star linebacker Kyle Weaver does. There's not much I can do about my looks, but I can bolster my image. And then, hopefully just like him, I can become a chick magnet. That way, I'll finally find a girl that will stick with me.

A beautiful woman walks toward me, one with red hair and a nice figure. I smile and make eye contact, something I've seen Kyle do when he talks to woman. I've learned I gotta make it clear that I'm interested.

But then she passes through the line and pays me absolutely zero mind. Embarrassed, I pull out my phone from my pocket and stare down at it, hoping that no one is watching my face go red.

Gosh darn it, man. I don't know what my problem is. It's like women see right through me. And even the few times I've been in a relationship, I can I tell it's going south before it even goes south. I can feel her withdraw, getting quiet and more distant. And then she breaks up with me, like they always do. I'm hoping that once I show how kind and philanthropic I can be with my increased NFO salary, I'll be irresistible and break-up-proof to women.

But there is the little phase I had back at Miss U that could explain it all. The one where I would fool around with the other guys on the football team—sometimes as a group, sometimes one-on-one. This included Kyle Weaver, today's Sexiest Man Alive. Of course, I would have never gotten the courage to do all this if it wasn't for Aaron Watkins. He was my chemistry tutor, the one who eventually introduced me to the concept of being gay. And the one who introduced me to gay sex. At this time, I thought I was gay, but now I see it as a distant phase, one I grew out of. I enjoyed it, though, and I know I should be grateful for all that he helped me see about myself. I sure as hell didn't learn about gay stuff growing up with Christian parents in Georgia. But the truth is, I'm still furious at that man for what he did to me.

He tutors me. Sweetens me up with his kind words. We become friends. Real good friends. So good of friends that we start kissing, touching each other. That's when he teaches me what it means to be gay, puts a name to all these wild feelings inside my chest. We have sex—make love, I insist on calling it with him. Because that's what it is. Love. We act like boyfriends in everything but name: sleepovers, dates, sex. He's the light of my life. And then he walks out on me, calls the whole thing off. And it's like it never happened. I mostly used sex with this other group of gay players as a way to get over him.

But I've since moved on, grown up from my gay phase. Yet even after all these years, I still can't forgive him for the hurt he caused me. He never even bothered to give more closure despite how many times I reached out. He just ignored me.

Part of me worries I'll see him here. Back in college, he told me how he wanted to go study cancer—leukemia I think. His sister died of the same disease when he was young, and he wanted to devote his life to ending it. I always thought him noble and kind for such an aspiration. Too bad he turned out to be a major dick—sorry, jerk. Maybe because he's such a jerk he changed career paths to something more selfish. Yeah, that's probably it. So I don't need to worry about seeing him here.

Then someone practically falls onto my back, and I feel something like a penis press into my butt. Even though it's soft, it's big enough for me to know that's what it is. I stumble forward, embarrassed even more, and I apologize, now seeing that the line has moved up and I held us in place. But when I turn around to see who just ran into me, I have to look twice and blink several times before I turn to fully face him. Because if I'm not hallucinating, the man who tore my heart into pieces is standing right in front of me.

"Hey, Dominic," he says. "Long time no see."

I scoff, and I feel the rage of just barely missing a tackle as I realize it really is the man who abandoned me. "You got some real nerve, man," I say. "Speaking to me as if nothing happened."

I can see the big man shrink inside himself a bit. Good. It'll give him a small dose of the dreadful feeling he gave me when he walked out.

"Look, I'm sorry," he says.

I let out a short, bitter laugh. "Sorry for what?"

He sighs and looks at the ground, his arms folded.

I hate to say it, but the man looks good. He's got that farmer's build just like me, and he looks like he's gotten more muscular. His hair is still that jet black, and I can see little whisps of gray on his sideburns, which I hate to admit make my knees a little weak. I've been told my strawberry blonde hair is what gets all the ladies, but that's empirically false. Of the two of us, Aaron's hair is definitely sexier, especially with the gray. The only thing I've got going for me is my three inches over him—height, that is—and the fact that I've probably got a good 30-50 pounds more muscle.

"I didn't—" he stutters. "I didn't know you'd be here."

I blow hot air out of my nose, my entire body so steaming angry that I'm sure I'm bright red right now. But I don't know what to say to this man. Because more than anything, I think I'm excited to see him. Almost relieved. Which makes no gosh darn sense at all.

"I can help the next guest," the woman at the hotel desk says.

Aaron's eyes move from me to the desk and back.

I step out of the way. "Go ahead of me," I say, my voice deadly calm. "It's not like you have any problem leaving me behind."

Aaron winces, which satisfies me, and he looks behind him. These academics and donors are too refined to be rude, but I can tell some of these people would cuss us out for holding up the line if they could.

He looks back at me. "Thanks," he says, then walks past me. And I'm furious that he actually does take my offer. Because I want an apology, gosh darn it. A conversation. Because, I think, for this whole stinking time, I've missed him badly. And he still won't give me the time of day.

Aaron approaches the counter, and I step up slowly behind me, trying to calm the raging emotions inside me. I remember seeing a counselor a couple years back who helped me process my grandpa dying. She said we feel our emotions in our bodies. At first, I thought it was hooey. But now I can't deny it. Because anger is so hot in my chest it feels like it'll burst.

The concierge says something and frowns at Aaron.

"Are you serious?" he asks, then shakes his head. I step up closer to hear what's going on.

"Laura Dennison," she says. "She was the one who changed your reservation?"

"Yes," Aaron says, calm and kind but clearly impatient.

She nods, then squints down at her computer. "This is so strange. You're sure she got you your own room?"

Aaron nods his head slowly. "She told me herself."

She shakes her head. "Let me get my manager."

She leaves for a minute, then returns with a blonde woman not much older than her. She looks at the computer, frowns, then stands up to address Aaron.

"I'm sorry sir, but it seems we've double-booked your room."

Aaron's jaw drops. "You're joking."

"I'm not," she says drily. "We've recently updated our system, and it looks like whoever rebooked your reservation got confused by the new interface and booked you over someone else."

"Oh man," he says, wiping his face. "Is there another room I can get?"

The manager looks down at the computer and clicks the mouse a few times. "We're booked solid with this conference. That's probably why you were double-booked in the first place. We can refund you, or give you credit for another stay."

Aaron runs his hands through his thick hair. I always enjoyed playing with it. Dang—what am I saying?

"I need to be here for this conference," he says. "And I can't stay elsewhere."

"Are you okay then with sharing this room with someone else?" she asks.

He lets out a short laugh. "Are there two beds?"

She looks down at the computer, then nods.

"And who is this other person?"

She squints down at the computer. "Dominic Johnson," she says.

I swear Kyle's face goes pale white, and all the heat leaves my body in an instant. I'm ice cold.

"Doesn't he play for the St. Louis Steamers?" the concierge asks.

I step forward. "I do," I say. "I'm Dominic Johnson."

"Well, Mr. Johnson," the manager says, folding her arms. "You heard everything. Are you willing to share a room with this man?"

I glance at Aaron, and he's just staring at the floor, his jaw locked.

I sigh. I don't want to go through the hassle of finding another place, and I definitely don't want to waste time commuting. I want to hear all the different cancer initiatives going on before I decide on the right one.

"Fine," I say.

Aaron whips his head to me. He looks angry, then his face melts into confusion.

"Dr. Watkins, is this okay with you?"

Doctor. Not only is Aaron one of the most beautiful men I know. He's got brains, too.

He rubs his temples, something he always did when he was thinking how to explain a difficult concept to me, and my chest gets all tight again. Not from anger, though, which is weird. It's more from a desire to pull him close and hold him tight so he can never run away from me again.

"Fine," he says. "Can we get our key cards?"

Chapter 3

Aaron Watkins

LAURA AND I WENT to see this indie musical about a father trying to win back the love of his ex-wife and estranged children. The song at the darkest, saddest point of the musical talked about how guilt burns you from the inside out, making you feel that kind of heat you feel on a summer's day, the one so hot that no shelter or water can cool you down.

And that's exactly how I feel right now.

As Dominic and I walk to the elevators to go up to our room—because of fucking course fate made us share a room—there's so much I want to say. I want to apologize for leaving him. I want to hear how he's been. I want to talk and laugh like we used to do.

But what would be the point?

The dude was playing football for Miss U, and he was destined to go on to the NFO. I would go to his games. He played like a beast, and he was setting records as a defensive tackle. If I didn't end it, then it was only going to be a matter of time before he would. There are no openly gay NFO players out there that I know of, and I doubted Dominic would be the first one.

And even if we did decide to stay together despite the whole sexuality thing, Dominic would have found some other reason to leave me. They always do. I mean, look at my parents. After Lorie, my sister, died from leukemia at age six, our steep medical bills sucked the life right out of my parents. Dad stayed around, but mom lost interest in me, and even then dad was a shadow of what he was. With my sister gone and the bills high, there was no reason to keep the family together. Or at least I wasn't a good enough reason.

Which is the root of the reason why I'm here in the first place. I don't want kids dying of leukemia, and I sure as hell don't want families getting torn apart because of it like mine was. That's why I want to find funding. I want to give future kids and families the life that Lorie could never have. That I could never have.

So no matter what kind of past we have, Dominic Johnson is not getting in the way of this. I haven't even let myself date *anyone* the past few years—it's too much of a distraction, and I want to focus on my research. Besides, I'm not gonna open my heart up to someone who could one day lose interest in me. He's a beautiful football player for Christ's sake. He could get any woman he wanted. His old, beefy flame should therefore be of no interest to him.

I press the elevator button, and we stand there, not knowing what to say or do. It's been nearly seven years after all.

"How's the NFO treating you?" I finally ask. I may not want to re-open our past, but I don't see why I can't be cordial.

I expect him to lash out at me like he did in the lobby, but when he sighs, I get the feeling that the worst of our conversations are behind us. Hopefully.

"Like a dream, man," he says, his slight Georgian accent coming through. I'm from Louisiana, but I toned down my accent by the time college came around. I kinda admire Dominic for being humble enough to keep a little bit of his.

I resist a grin as I look up at him. "How so?" I ask. I don't want to fall back into our old friendship either, no matter how easy it was. Dominic and I are better off without each other.

"Oh, you know," he says with a shrug. "It's like it was in college: football, beer, friends. Except the stakes are higher now."

Other people are also waiting for the elevator, but he talks loudly like it's just the two of us. I always loved how he was just like a big, clumsy dog: friendly, eager, funny, attention-grabbing. And not to mention how well he's aged. Goddamn. It's not just his ass that I admire. His chest is wide and thick, and his arms look too big for his hoodie sleeves. He has this absolutely perfect strawberry blonde hair that stands out against his pale complexion, while my hair is already starting to gray. I wish I had his color. He's like a brash, handsome farm-boy you get a crush on if you were to go work on a secluded ranch for the summer. Fun for a time, but then you have to let him go. Except I didn't account for the fact that this cute farm-boy could reappear in my life seven years later.

The elevator doors open, and we all crowd inside. I get in the far back corner, and I expect Dominic, especially with how angry he was earlier, to stand on opposite end. But instead, he stands right next to me. So close that I can smell his signature earthy musk mixed with his deodorant. God, I've missed this smell. And it's only gotten better since I've last seen him, like whiskey aging in a barrel.

More and more people pile in, squishing us all together, and I have to resist a shiver that Dominic's touch sends throughout my body. Soon, we're pressed closer and closer together, until finally Dominic's ass is pressed right against the crotch of my slacks. I try prop my ass up on the handrail to thus get further away from his perfect Georgia peaches, but all this does is raise me higher until I'm practically spooning him.

"It's leukemia research you do, right?" he asks as the doors are closing. There's some mild chatter, but I'm still much too self-conscious to talk about anything with how quiet it is. Especially considering that there are probably other academics in here who know vastly more than I do.

"Alrighty then," Dominic says when I don't reply, and I roll my eyes. I'll answer when we're alone.

When we're alone.

I still can't believe we're sharing a room.

When we reach our floor, Dominic manages to part the crowd like the red sea, wide enough for both of us to pass through with ease. I guess being a huge football player has its advantages.

"Room 63," Dominic says, looking at his phone.

I nod. "And yes," I say. "It is leukemia research."

"Cool," he says as we walk. He seems relieved I actually answered him. "You were always a smart one."

My chest warms at that. I want to say that there's sarcasm there, but Dominic has never been one to lie. If he's angry, he'll show it. If he's sad, he'll show it. If he's giving me a compliment—which he is—then he means it.

We reach our room, and Dominic opens the door for us. He walks in and turns on the lights while I adjust my carry-on. But when I look up at him, he gawks like he's seen a dead body.

"What's wrong?" I ask.

He doesn't reply as I rush into the room. Because he doesn't need to. I see exactly why he's paralyzed.

There's only one queen bed.

I can't help but break into a laugh. It's all I have the energy to do at this point. And that's when Dominic starts laughing with me, his big booming chuckle rattling my chest.

Both smiling, we lock eyes, and for a moment I remember why I loved being around him so much. The man is unfailingly positive and has enough genuine energy to power the entire city of New York.

"Guess we can't get another room," he says. "Them being all occupied and all."

I let go of my suitcase and rub my eyes, realizing just how tired I am. I've spent the whole day traveling, and the summer sun's just set outside the window.

"I think you're right," I say, plopping down on the bed. "I don't even think I have the energy to fight for a new room or refund. Just wish they didn't lie about it."

He plops down on the bed, and my body becomes aware of just how close he is.

"Don't think they lied," he says with a shrug. "Seems like they're genuinely just overwhelmed with the conference and their new system."

Calm and understanding like he always was. *Fuck.*

The two of us sit there, only a couple feet apart. But the distance also feels achingly long, like there's nothing in the universe that could close the gap. Except if I were to maybe let myself just open back up to him.

Nope.

I have room for no one in my life, especially not Dominic Johnson.

I jump to my feet, feeling the heat under the gaze of his icy blue eyes.

"I should shower," I say. "Been traveling all day."

He stretches and leans back. "Have at it. I'm beat, so I'm gonna get into bed."

Into the bed we're going to share.

"Alrighty," I say, my forehead breaking into a sweat.

Dominic grabs the collar of his shirt to take it off, and I take that as a sign for me to go. I speed into the bathroom before I catch sight of just how much more muscled he's become, and I close the door with a breath of relief. I turn on the shower, and the sound of running water calms my racing thoughts.

Of all people, Dominic and I are the ones the hotel system randomly put in the same room? *With one bed?*

I step into the hot shower and try, unsuccessfully, to relax.

Christ—Dominic looks so much better than I remember—so much more muscular and confident. I guess that's what a career in the NFO will do to you. But what's even more surprising is that he's maintained his sweet, fun-loving demeanor. Wouldn't he be disillusioned with the NFO by now? With life? I know I am with my career. I can't believe I make it all the way to an assistant professorship, only to have the rug ripped from under me when my senior mentor compromises our research funds. It's like the universe is mocking me. I'm trying to help people so they don't have to go through what me and my family went through. So why am I being punished for someone else's actions by being forced to room with the man I used to fuck?

After taking my time in the shower, hoping that by now Dominic will be fast asleep, I get out and dry myself. And then my stomach sinks to the floor.

I forgot to bring in a change of clothes.

Which means I have to walk out of this bathroom with only a towel as cover and retrieve my clothes from my suitcase. Let's just pray Dominic's already asleep.

When I crack open the door, the lights are still on, and I curse to myself. He has to be awake.

Or maybe he left the lights on for me.

Whatever. I either grab my clothes or get in the bed naked. And I am *not* doing that.

I sheepishly tiptoe over to suitcase sitting out in the open. And out of the corner of my eye, the man is in bed leaning against the headboard. *Shirtless.* And he's reading a book.

He looks up at me, and his eyes trail down my torso to the towel around me waist. He stares at it as his look alone could tear the towel from my waist.

No. Dominic Johnson's a defensive tackle in the NFO. So, even if he is gay, he wouldn't get with me again. He has a job to maintain. Letting my mind wander about what he could be thinking about me, though tempting, is therefore useless.

I crouch down and open my suitcase, eager to get some clothes on. On the far end of the room, the air conditioner's blasting, and I'm already shivering.

After I grab some pajamas, I glance up at him, and he immediately looks down at his book as if he's embarrassed I caught him eyeing me. The silence between us thick enough to choke, I go into the bathroom to change into my pajamas. When I return, there's a special kind of awkward between us, like were both strongly attracted magnets and the force keeping us apart is too much to resist. Like were *holding* magnets, I should say. I don't want to insinuate that Dominic and I are meant for each other or anything. But it's awkward nonetheless, so I ask an innocuous question to ease the tension.

"Whatcha reading?" I ask, unable to see the book clearly.

He sets the book down and rubs his eyes while yawning, giving me a full view of his torso. Christ Almighty. The man looks like he's made of pure protein and spends every waking moment working out. His bodies filled out since college, and his light brown chest hair gilds his pecs like the drapes adorning a stage at a Broadway show. I want to run my hands through it and feel just how hard those muscles are. And that's definitely not the only hard thing I want to feel.

Aaron, no. Even if Dominic was somehow into me, it could never work. And besides, I can't do relationships right now. leukemia research is more important.

He releases his hands from his face. "You know Freida McFadden?"

"Yeah," I say. "Thriller author?"

He laughs. "Yeah, kinda obsessed with her. This is her third book about a housemaid."

I laugh with him. "That's awesome."

And my chest tingles at that. It's like... cute that he's reading. And mature? I don't know. When I began tutoring him, I thought he was the douchey frat bro type. But the more I got to know him, the more I wanted to hold him against my body and protect him against every single thing that could ever hurt him.

Except for me, of course. I couldn't protect him from myself.

Exhausted, and not able to put it off any longer, I walk over to my side of the bed and get the covers. It's already so warm underneath because of Dominic's body heat. Lord help me.

"I'll try my best to say on my side," he says, setting his book down on the nightstand. He stretches, showing off his tree-trunk-sized arms. "I know I'm a big guy."

"Alright," I say, trying not to think about just how big he is. I attempt to make myself comfortable as far away from him as possible.

"Goodnight," he says. "And I'm sorry for snapping at you down there. It's good to see you again."

I sigh, my back to him. "It's all good," I say. "It's really good to see you too."

We both shut our lights off, and I'm actually grateful for the loud AC blasting. Because it's loud enough to drown out my brain screaming at me that the NFO player I may still have feelings for is laying right next to me.

* * *

I wake up in a panic. It's pitch-black, and I'm shivering so hard that I'm afraid I'll crack my teeth.

"Woah, woah," I hear Dominic say. His warm hand touches my waist. "Dang, Aaron. You're freezing."

"Y-yeah," I say. "A-AC." I can hear it blasting even harder now, and for some reason, I'm only half-covered by the duvet.

"Do you want me to turn it off?" he asks.

I try to answer, but I'm too tired and cold to get the words out.

"Here," he says. He pulls me toward him and presses me against his warm body, and it feels like I've just jumped into a hot tub. He wraps his huge arms around me, swaddling me like a babe in a blanket, and pulls the duvet over us. Gradually, my shivering subsides, and I feel Dominic's warm breath on the back of my neck.

And his thick cock hardening against my ass.

Suddenly, I'm wide awake.

I know I should be pushing him off me and thus protecting the both of us from love that could never work.

But I can't. Because, truth be told, I feel safer here in his arms. More than I have in the past seven years. Like my worth isn't dependent on some project getting funded or finished, like I'm just inherently good and have nothing to worry about. So, at the very least, I'm letting myself have this feeling for one night.

I nuzzle against his hard cock, and he holds me tighter.

I think we're both too tired for any funny business. I'd definitely stop us before it got to that, anyways. But, feeling just how hard he is, I'm reassured that I may not be the only one with residual feelings.

Chapter 4

Dominic Johnson

WHEN I WAKE UP, my length feels so good that I tighten my arms around whatever I'm holding and thrust. I hear a moan, and whatever is making my rod feel good presses harder against it, and I'm worried I'll bust right here.

And that's when I remember I'm in the same bed as Aaron Watkins, the first man and person I ever had sex with.

My eyes shoot open, and the first thing I see is the back of Aaron's head. I try to pull away, but Aaron is clutching my arms to his chest like his left depends on it. Which means I can't really move my manhood away from him even if I tried.

Memories of last night then hit me. The poor man was shivering to death. I couldn't just lay there and do nothing. But I didn't need to shove my manhood against his butt.

He adjusts himself against me, increasing the pressure against my shaft even more, and I have to hold in a moan.

I can't be doing this. Aaron Watkins tore my heart into a million pieces. And even if he didn't, I'm over this gay stuff. I'm here to find a worthy cancer project to fund so I can't get some good press attention and hopefully attract a girl who will want me. Because I'm a straight man now.

Carefully, I find where his hands grip me and try to pull him off without waking him. Which is harder than I think. Aaron's gotten more muscular since I've last seen him. And that doesn't make my boner situation any easier.

Eventually, I loosen his grip, allowing me to disentangle our limbs. Then, I slide away from him and stand up. My penis is so hard my shorts look like a black teepee, and I think I'm even leaking some precum. Aaron shifts in his sleep, so I rush into the bathroom before he sees how hard he's made me.

I turn on the shower and get in once it's warm, but my penis is still ramrod straight. I can still feel Aaron's hairy back against me, how wonderful my manhood felt pressing into his butt even with both our clothes getting in the way.

When Aaron and I did the deed back in college, he tended to be the one to put it inside me. That's just the way we were then, and that felt easier. But I've learned a few things since. And now I want to be the one who makes him moan and breaks his back.

What the heck am I thinking? I'm here for one purpose and one purpose only. Aaron Watkins will not be a distraction.

But as I stare down at my shaft that is still as hard as a rock, I know I'll have to get rid of this particular distraction.

I start stroking myself, thinking of all the beautiful women I've seen in the past week, including that redhead in the lobby yesterday. But my mind keeps going back to Aaron like a ball rolling down a hill.

I lean back against the shower tiles, let the water run down my torso, and sigh. I may not be gay now, and I sure as heck am not letting myself fall for Aaron again, but I can still pleasure myself with the thought of him. There can't be harm in that.

When I picture how he looked in that towel last night and remember how he felt in my arms, it doesn't take me long. Which hacks me off. Because it's so easy with him on my mind, way easier than thinking about women.

And come to think of it, it was always so easy with him. He was thoughtful, always concerned about how my practices and games were going. How I was doing in school. All my friends loved to party. But Aaron was more than that. He liked to party, but he also liked to go on walks and talk about deep subjects and stupid things. He loved singing along to musicals, and he also liked to cook for me. He was a man of substance, and the more I was around him, the more I wanted to dig into him and get to know him better.

I know I'm straight now and have moved on from all this gay stuff. But is it really so bad for me to want to be around a person like that? If not as a partner, then as a friend?

I finish my shower and then get ready for the opening session. If I want to find the right project to fund, I want to look my best. Once I've freshened up, I leave the bathroom to put my suit on. And Aaron's awake.

I want to be cold with him. I want to push him away so nothing happens between us, and I want to make him hurt for all he's done to me.

But I can't for the life of me.

Because I still care about this man. And at the very least, I do think I want us to be friends.

"Hey, man," I say. "You sleep good?"

He flashes me a small smirk, then wipes it from his face. Right. If anything, I should know how he slept. Because he was in my arms.

"Good," he says, sitting on the edge of the bed. His eyes flicker between me and my torso. "You headed to the opening session?"

"Yep," I say. "I can save you a seat if you'd like."

He pauses for a moment, thinking. "Thanks. I had plans to sit with my friend Laura, but I'll let you know."

"Alright," I say. *Not like you both can't sit with me,* I want to say. But there's no use in starting a silly fight this early in the morning.

I take my suit clothing into the bathroom and get dressed. I walk out to grab my phone before leaving.

Aaron, getting his clothes ready, stops and looks at me. And I swear he's checking me out.

"Bathroom's all yours," I say adjusting my tie, not unhappy to snag his gaze. "See you around."

But Aaron says nothing as I shut the door behind me. Sheesh. It doesn't cost anything to be kind. Guess being friends with Aaron may not work out after all.

Once I'm down in the main conference area, I check in and put the conference lanyard around my neck. Then I get some breakfast from the buffet and sit down at a nearby table. The room is already bustling with donors, academics, and researchers. Looks like I'll have plenty of options to choose from.

Right as I take a bite of some juicy sausage, somebody taps me on the back. With the sausage in my mouth, I immediately think it's Aaron, but I get that image out of my head as quickly as possible. Midchew, I look up to see my old friend from Miss U, Kyle Weaver.

"What's up," I say, standing up and giving my old friend a hug.

He pulls away and taps me on the shoulders. "The best defensive tackle ever to grace the St. Louis Steamers," he says. "How the hell are ya?"

My face turns red from his compliment. Kyle Weaver was one of the most well-known guys that was part of the underground faction of gay Miss U football players, mostly because of what a kind man he was. And certainly how handsome he was too. Well, is. He just got selected as People's Sexiest Man Alive.

He and I even fooled around a few times, even when my heart was still aching for Aaron Watkins. But he and I are friends now, and were I actually into men, he wouldn't really interest me. Not so much my type anymore. Besides, most guys as part of this faction agreed that we wouldn't come onto each other while playing in the NFO, and we all agreed to keep each others' identities as secret as possible.

"I'm good man," I say. "You know, I got a raise this past year."

"Congrats," he says, his Mississippi accent strong.

"Thanks," I say. "Just here looking for some good to do with it."

"Oh, that's amazing, man," he says. "Good for you. I have to say it's fulfilling as hell, especially having lost my daddy to pancreatic cancer."

"My condolences as always," I say.

"Much obliged," he says. "But you're in the right place if you wanna find a good cause. You can't really go wrong here."

I spot Aaron walking over to the check-in table, and I lose my train of thought. He's wearing an eye-popping navy suit that makes his dark hair and beard almost look purple. And it fits him in all the right places. It even looks a little too tight, like he gained some muscle after he'd already been fitted for it. But he looks like a dream.

"You good?" Kyle asks.

I blink twice. "Oh yeah, sorry about that. Just tired." *Even though I had some of the best sleep of my life with my arms wrapped around Aaron.*

"Well good luck finding something worthwhile," Kyle says, tapping me on the back. "Like I said, you can't go wrong."

"Thanks man. Hopefully see you around."

And with that, Kyle Weaver is gone, only to be swiftly replaced by Aaron Watkins.

His cologne wafts over to me, and he smells like leather and cedar. Gosh darn it man. If Aaron was a woman, I'd be all over him.

"I thought you were sitting with your friend," I say. I try to sound bitter, begrudging. But I just come off like I'm excited that he might sit with me. Because I am excited.

"Change of plans," he says. "My friend Laura from grad school is pregnant, and she's got some bad morning sickness. I'll be surprised if she makes it out by noon."

I wince. "Yikes. Sorry to hear that."

He shrugs his big shoulders. "It's whatever. Your offer still open to sit together?"

I resist smiling with all the strength I have, and I think I'm mostly successful. "Only if you can get me some more sausage."

His face blanches, and I sigh.

"Breakfast sausage, I mean."

"Alright," he says, playing with one of the buttons on his suit coat. "Sure."

By the time he's back, I'm almost done with my plate, and I know I'll need seconds, so I'm grateful for the sausage that Aaron drops onto my plate. It lands with a thunk, and I immediately think about my own sausage pressed against Aaron's cheeks. I have to hold in a cough.

By now, the coordinators for the event have started speaking, but Aaron and I are far enough away to where it still feels like we can just talk casually. He takes one of those syrup packets and proceeds to pour it not only over his pancake but also over his eggs, bacon and sausage too.

"Oh man," I say, grimacing and laughing at the same time. "You still do that, huh?"

"What?" he asks defensively. But the corner of his mouth is turned upward. "I like sweet and savory."

I chuckle. "Reminds me of that breakfast casserole you used to make me before my Saturday games," I say. "So savory and spicy with the eggs, mushrooms, sausage, and jalapeno. And then you'd ruin your slice with some syrup."

Aaron's chewing as I wait for his reply, but then I get nervous. What if he doesn't want to talk about the past? What if I scare him away again like I do with every other girl?

He swallows. "Oh, don't even start with me there," he says.

And my chest clenches. Great. I have scared him away.

"Because you and I both know that made it taste better. You even said so yourself."

I laugh, more relieved than anything. Turns out I didn't scare him, and we can talk normally. Good.

"Yeah, it was tasty for a bite or two," I say. "But if I want savory, I want savory. If I want sweet, I want sweet. Maybe I'll mix the two on Thanksgiving or something. But all the time?" I smirk at him. "You'd have to be crazy."

"Maybe I am," he says, making a gesture of eating his syrup-soaked eggs. "But I am plenty satisfied."

Really? I want to ask. *Because I think I can satisfy you better.*

I shake the dirty thoughts from my head. Aaron and I will be friends. Nothing more.

"Well, I'll admit," I say. "Your cooking was phenomenal, whether it was sweet, savory, or both. Hope I didn't offend you by slamming your tastes."

"Not at all," Aaron says. "And thanks. I always forget how much I enjoy cooking until someone compliments me on it."

"The compliments are well deserved," I say, looking at him with a smile. He blushes, which makes me blush, so we both look away from each other. Am I flirting with Aaron Watkins? I told myself we'd just be friends.

To distract myself from my anxious thoughts, I sneak up to get another plate while the keynote speaker is talking. Once I'm back, Aaron looks like he wants to say something.

"You know what," he says.

"What?" I ask. But I don't say more. This is like when a shy cat that you've been trying to pet finally approaches you. You have to stay still so you don't scare it. Likewise, I don't want to do or say anything to stop him from talking.

"I really miss football season," he says. "Living through it, that is. The crisp fall scent just before a football game, apple cider, pumpkin patches, chili, and beer. And it was cool living the season with a football player like yourself."

My whole body tingles. Is Aaron Watkins saying that he misses me? Because him bringing all this up makes me miss those times as well. And my time with him.

"It was grand," I say, smiling as I recollect. "Chilling together after a game."

"Watching a relaxing movie afterwards to wind down," he says.

"Or a horror movie," I say. "Which wouldn't wind you down."

He laughs. "And massaging your sore muscles."

And neither of us say the next thing. We just stare into each other's eyes. Because we're both thinking it, but we're too scared to say it. Because those massage sessions always turned into something a lot more... intimate.

"Good times," I say.

"Sure were," he says.

Then why'd you leave me? I want to ask. But I don't want to ruin the moment and scare him away. So just I bask in the warmth of the conversation.

"So why are you here?" he asks. "Sorry if that's rude."

I shrug. I don't want to tell him the truth and come off as some Johnny Bravo hunk who's too incompetent to get laid.

So I act like Johnny Bravo and try to make myself look good.

"Too much money to know what to do with," I say. "Want to donate to a good cause."

His brow furrows. "Really?"

"Yeah," I say. "Is that weird or something?"

"No," he says, shaking his head. "That's... nice."

"And why are you here?" I ask.

He lets out a self-deprecating laugh. "I'm looking for funding."

Now I furrow my brow. "Funding? How so?"

He sighs. "You ready for this?"

I tilt my chair to him. "Lay it on me."

And so he tells me the story about how his tenured mentor was embezzling funds from Admiral University in Iowa, mixing them with his own grants and research funds, which put all the money under investigation, barring Aaron from using any of it just when he was hired on to use these funds to do key leukemia research in children.

I blow air through my lips. "Damn. That's brutal. I'm sorry."

He lets out a nervous laugh. "Tell me about it. And this conference is my last chance to get funding. If I don't, then I might as well quit. Because they won't give me tenure if this research doesn't take off."

There's an ache in my chest, and I reach under my tie to rub it.

Aaron needs funding, and I have money. Leukemia research is as important as ever. And in children? That's a perfect cause to support and get a woman attracted to me. But would Aaron want a professional relationship with me? Would I be able to keep it professional with him?

The keynote speaker ends, and the entire room claps. Aaron and I quickly join the praise even though we've paid no attention. Folks stand up, and the first round of presentations begin in less than ten minutes. This will be a jam-packed weekend.

Aaron stands up. "I should be going."

"When do you present?" I ask. "I'll come."

"I don't present until Sunday morning," he says, straightening his tie. "But I want to talk to people and build some connections. Hopefully find the person to fund me."

"Of course," I say.

He looks down at his chair, then below it. Then he looks around the table, growing more frantic by the second.

"You all good?" I ask.

"My briefcase," he says. "I had it in my carry-on. I know I brought it on this trip. It has copies of my CV and research plan. If I don't have it, I won't be able to leave info with potential investors." He runs his hands through his hair, freezes, then sighs. "Fuck. I think I left it in the room. Sorry for swearing."

"Don't worry about me," I say. I don't like to swear, but other people can do what they want. It's sweet of Aaron to consider me even when he's stressed.

"Go get it," I say. "You still have some time."

"Right," he says. And then he's off.

And I try to be thoughtful toward Aaron during this stressful time, but I can't help but watch his butt bounce as he runs out of the conference room.

Chapter 5

Aaron Watkins

How could I be so stupid? Forgetting my bag on the first day of the most important conference of my life? I rush to the elevator, making small, quick strides so I don't rip my pants.

After my sister died—and after my family steadily grew apart—I made a promise to myself. I made a promise that I would seek to undo the pain that happened to our family. I promised to help end leukemia and all the suffering that comes with it, both personally and in the family. And what do I do when my entire career in the field is on the line? I forget my fucking briefcase.

I know what my dad would say: this isn't something you really care about, is it? To which I would reply: I'm trying. And I am trying. I just wish that my parents could have been there to help me after Lorie died. I was suffering too. But they just left me to wallow and raise myself on my own. And now, I'm an adult on my own. I haven't spoken to either of them in years. My wish, this whole time, has been to conduct groundbreaking research. To find something to cure this awful disease. Maybe then mom and dad will finally love me. Maybe then they'll love me enough to bring the family back together.

By the time I reach floor six, I'm nearly in tears, but I don't know why. I know my bag is in here, and the worst is I make it to a session slightly late. So why is my chest hurting so much it feels like it'll rip in two?

When I get to my door, I reach back into my suit pocket for my wallet.

But it isn't there.

And that's when I remember I didn't feel the lump when I sat down to eat with Kyle. So I left my wallet, with my key card, in my hotel room.

I bang my fist against the door and press my forehead against it. Thoughts of self-hatred swim in my head. I know I should call my therapist to talk about this. But I'm so angry that I can't even think about anything beyond my stupid key card and briefcase.

Then I freeze, my eyes widening.

I do have a roommate—a *bedmate* for fuck's sake. And he likely has his keycard. He was always mindful of little details like that in college. I may have walked out on him, but that doesn't mean he won't help me, right?

Right?

Pressing my forehead against the door, I realize I have no other option. I pull out my phone and find his contact. After I ended things, I blocked him so I wouldn't be tempted to go back, but I never deleted his number. I couldn't bring myself to do it. So, I unblock him, press the call button, and put the phone to my ear.

He answers on the first ring. "Aaron?" he asks as if this the first time we've spoken in seven years.

"I left my key card in my room," I say, my eyes watering, trying not to be moved by the concern in his voice. "Can you help?"

"I'll be right there," he says. And then he hangs up.

I stand there against the door with my arms folded, trying my best to keep my tears back. But they leak out like I'm some old, defunct faucet. And I don't know why. I know where my items are, and I'm about to get them back. It's not like they're lost forever.

Sooner than I would expect, I hear the elevator ding, and I see Dominic with his pristine gray suit jog off the elevator. He reaches our door without a word and puts the card up to the reader. It dings and flashes green, and a knot of tension releases in my shoulders.

"Thank you," I say, pushing the door open as I rush inside.

And there they are. My briefcase is sitting on a lonely chair with my wallet right next to it. I rush to it and unzip it to assess the contents. And everything's accounted for.

So why are there still fresh tears streaming down my face?

The door shuts behind me, and I expect Dominic to be gone. But when I turn my head, he's standing right in front of the bed with his hands in his pockets.

"You don't need to stay here with me," I say, wiping my eyes. "I'm fine. Just go."

There's a pause, but I don't hear him move.

"Stop pushing me away," he says.

I turn to him, my chest tightening. He's staring at me with those big blue eyes and that gorgeous, rugged face.

And that's when I break into a sob.

He opens his arms. "Come here."

And I rush into him like he's my home. He embraces me, and we sit down on the bed. I wail into his shirt, grabbing it with both my hands. I feel bad that I'm ruining this amazing suit, but Dominic has his arms wrapped around me, holding me against him, so I couldn't move if I tried. And I let out all the tears. Because I feel safe doing so.

"I'm here," he says, stroking my back. "I'm here, Aaron."

That makes me cry harder. Because besides Laura, he's really the only one who has been a consistent friend to me. Not friend—family. That's how we were at Miss U. Dominic Johnson was my practically my boyfriend, my family. And I abandoned him. Just like my parents did to me.

"Why?" I say into his shirt.

"'Why' what?" he asks.

I pull away from him and look up into his blue eyes. "Why did they leave me?" I ask. "And why did I go get this stupid Ph.D. in cancer biology just to study leukemia, only to lose my funding right when I could actually do research that could benefit the field? Right when I could finally prove my parents that I'm worthy of being loved?"

He looks at me like I'm crazy. "What are you saying?"

I try to pull away from him, but his arms still keep me close.

"Aaron, what is going on?" he asks.

"It doesn't matter," I say. "I'm just being crazy."

"No you're not," he says. "You're talking about your parents. You hardly ever do that unless something serious happens."

"Because they're basically dead to me."

"But if they really were, would you be this upset about them now?"

I look up at him, a grimace forming on my face. "I just—" I hold back a sob. "I just thought that they would appreciate me if I could work at undoing what happened with Lorie."

"Are you saying you're going to cure cancer?"

I let out a sharp laugh. "Well when you put it that way..."

"I mean, you could," he says. "I remember you're that smart. You helped me pass chemistry after all. And that's a miracle in itself."

I roll my eyes, but I can't help but smile. Fucking Dominic always knows what to say.

"But what you're actually saying is impossible. You're saying you want to go back in time and undo what happened to Lorie. No one can do that."

Another sob comes on, and this time I can't hold it back. So I let the tears flow. Because he's right.

"So what?" I ask. "I'll never have my parents love?"

He shrugs. "I can't answer that," he says. "And I don't think anyone can."

I sniffle and wipe my eyes.

"But that was their choice to abandon you," he says. "You were a kid. You needed their love. You couldn't have done anything wrong."

I nod and let out a shaky sigh. "So all of this is for nothing then."

His brow forms a deep V. "Nothing? How is studying cancer nothing?"

"I'm not saying it's nothing, I just—"

"But you are. You're saying earning your parent's love is all that matters. But you can't earn it. Love is just given, Aaron. And that's the point. You're giving your love to the world—to all these families suffering from leukemia—by doing this research. You're doing the exact opposite of what your parents did. When your sister died, you've mentioned in the past that financial trouble and grief were so bad that they curled into themselves. But you blossomed outwards. You dedicated yourself to helping others. Sure, you wanted to earn your parents love, but the motivation to help was there. That sure as hell should count for something."

My eyes widen. "You swore."

"Which I only do when I'm trying to make an important point," he says. "Because you're a damn good man, Aaron Watkins. And I won't let anyone say otherwise. Not your parents. And especially not yourself."

More tears fall, but they aren't as much from sadness or anger or confusion this time. I pull myself closer to Dominic until our faces are only inches apart.

This man is more perfect than I imagined. Even after walking out on him, he can still sit and tell me what I need to hear. Seven years later, too. This isn't someone who wouldn't abandon me like my parents did, right?

He closes the distance between us, but I go all the way. I press my lips against his, and he lets out a deep moan. I hold it there for a minute, then I pull away.

"Sorry," I say.

"Don't you dare say you're sorry," he says. "You have no idea how much I've missed this."

I smile, then check my watch. We're almost through the first session, and the next one will start in fifteen.

I try to stand up, and Dominic lets me by unwrapping his arms.

I wipe my face. "I should go," I say. "To the next session. To find someone to fund me."

Kyle rubs his face and nods. "Right, uh. I should too."

"Right."

I walk over to grab my wallet and bag as Dominic stands and stretches.

He mentioned he's looking to fund a good cause. But could that cause be me? Surely not. We'd inevitably fall back into our relationship. Then he'd get scared because he plays for the NFO and could lose his career. Then he'd run away just like mom and dad, leaving me, yet again, without funding.

"Thanks for everything you've said," I say. "It's helped."

"Of course," he says. "Anytime. And I mean it."

"Thanks," I say, sheepishly. And I rush out of that room before I can even think of planting my lips on his again.

Chapter 6

Dominic Johnson

How is it that every time Aaron touches my body I get a hard-on?

I was going to follow Aaron out in the hallway because I also have sessions to attend, and I wanted to ensure that he was okay. But that would mean walking around the hotel looking like I'm carrying a sock in my pants. So, I'm standing next to our bed in our room until my length decides to soften.

Man, I can't believe Aaron and I kissed. I don't know what possessed me, but with him that close, I couldn't resist. Even though he is a man. In fact, I think I want to have him be *my* man.

No. That's not why I came here. I came to make myself likable enough for a woman to date me. Still don't know how being a defensive tackle in the NFO isn't good enough for a woman to like me, but that's whatever.

So I can't date a man, even if he is someone as beautiful and kind as Aaron. I play for the NFO. That kinda stuff isn't accepted in this world. And I love football. I can't just give that up.

I rub my forehead and check the schedule I got down in the conference room. There's a bunch of different sessions I could go to, but the most appealing is the one about the latest news in breast cancer. That could land me a woman, right? If I helped fund breast cancer research? I don't see anything on the schedule that could be any better. So, once I'm finally soft, I make my way down to the first floor and find the room where this breast cancer session is taking place.

But the entire time this woman is presenting her research, I can't stop thinking about Aaron. I remember how sour his mood turned whenever his parents came up. Holidays and breaks were always especially hard for him. He said those were the times that people would go home to see their families, while he just looked for excuses to stay on campus. I always told him that he could come home with me and visit my folks for Thanksgiving or Christmas. We'd have to pretend to be friends of course, but my parents were always welcoming to any friends of mine.

Yet he always turned me down. Said he'd rather get caught up on his studies, which never made sense because he was always on top of all his assignments and work. And since he's left me, after all these years, I thought he'd at least gotten some distance away from it all. But it looks like it's hurting him now more than ever.

I always consoled him as much as I could. I really hope he took in what I said earlier. 'Cause I meant every word.

Once the presentation's over, I make my way to talk to the lady. I had a hard time paying attention, but I did pick up some important bits. I want to see if she would like to meet further to discuss her specific needs.

But I'm not the only one.

Several others, somehow dressed nicer than me, get in line before I do. And they butter this woman up, telling her what a fantastic job she did, referencing other researchers and terms I don't recognize. Each person in front of me sets a time to meet with this woman, so many that this woman could have multiple sources of funding if she wanted to. She doesn't need inexperienced me. So, once I'm only one person away from speaking to her, I quietly bow out of line and rush for the exit. Once I'm out in the hallway, I lean against the wall and pull out my phone to look like I know what I'm doing, meanwhile kicking myself the entire time.

What on earth am I really trying to do here? The investors here are older, more experienced, and way richer than I am. Plus, I'm just some bonehead NFO player. What business do I have getting involved in cancer research this important? Sure, Kyle Weaver does it, but that's because he's Kyle Weaver. He's hot and confident. But I'm just some lug who can't land a woman if he tried.

I sigh, then pull out the schedule again. Maybe this was just a particularly good presentation, and that's why there were so many other donors more polished than me. I shouldn't give up yet. There is a session during the next block about ovarian cancer, something that could work just as well for my image. So I make my way there.

But this presentation is somehow worse.

Well, not technically worse. It's flawless as far as I can tell. But worse because watching the presentation makes me feel even more like a fish out of water.

The professor somehow manages to turn dry statistics into a compelling story, keeping all of us on the edge of our seats. And by the end, practically half the room gets up to talk to her. I don't even bother getting in line.

The next presentation about skin cancer is no different, and I'm so hungry at that point that I can hardly pay attention. When it's over, not even bothering to talk to the researcher, I rush to the main conference room so I can finally eat. And maybe so I can chat more with Aaron. Talking to him this morning was like stepping into air conditioning on a hot day. And kissing him was like...

Okay, I gotta stop thinking about that kiss. And that's not only because I can't date him. It's because he has the tendency to dip out just when things get important. Look at this morning: after we kiss, he runs away. No lingering, no talking, no apology about the past—just fleeing. Even after I held him in my arms and gave him all the sweet words I could.

As I get in line for the buffet, I think back on all the other ways Aaron's let me down, and anger boils inside my chest.

The way Aaron ended things in college was far worse than this morning. I remember it vividly. After my coach gives me the good news, I rush home to tell Aaron that NFO scouts are coming to my next game and that its likely I'll be drafted. And next thing I know, Aaron's sitting me down, telling me we need to break up. He gives no explanation—just says we can't work out. And then he takes his things and leaves my apartment. And I never hear from him again.

Gosh, I'm ridiculous. Walking through the buffet line, getting all teary eyed about a man who broke my heart so many years ago. When I was just a kid, too. I should be over this by now. I grew past this. But gosh darn it, now that I'm really thinking about all that happened, I don't really think I grew past this at all. I just stuffed it down.

When I get my food, I know I should sit down at another table and get to know other people, make connections and whatever. That's what I see Kyle Weaver doing over on the far side of the room.

But that's the last thing I want to do. In fact, the only thing I want to do is eat in silence and then go up to my room and nap.

As I eat, I mull over what I said to Aaron. Maybe I said something offensive to make him leave so quickly, even though I clearly know I didn't. He left of his own volition.

But that's when the truth dawns on me, and this truth doesn't just illuminate Aaron's weird behavior. It explains this whole event and my behavior.

Since his parents left him, Aaron's been carrying this wound, thinking he's inadequate and that he has to prove his worth or whatever by gaining their love back. And this entire time, I've been doing the exact same thing.

Here I am, thinking that I've moved on from my gay phase—that I can just find a girl and get married and live the life that a southern man like me is supposed to live. Of course, I decide to do this after Aaron breaks my heart. So, just like him, I brashly move on from the heartache he caused me, thinking that by finding a girl and forgetting about it all I can heal and feel worthy again.

But, just like I told Aaron, that doesn't work.

Which means I have to face the truth.

I, very much so, have not moved on from my gay phase. In fact, I don't even think it's a phase at all. And—more importantly—I am still very much in love with Aaron Watkins, the first man and person I was ever intimate with.

Suddenly, mid-chew with chicken tikka masala in my mouth, I lose all my appetite, and I feel the dull throb of a headache come on in between my eyebrows. I get up and throw my food away, then immediately head to the elevators. I need to lay down, stat.

By the time I'm fumbling with my key card at my hotel room door, my vision is getting spotty—the beginning stages of a migraine, and my tie and suitcoat are already off and hanging over my shoulder.

Once I'm inside, I thank God that the room is blissfully cold, tear my clothes off, and hide under the covers. Which still, annoyingly, smell very much like Aaron.

* * *

I wake to the door clicking shut. My eyes shoot open, and it takes me a moment to remember where I am. Taking in the beige hotel room, I remember I'm in New York City for the cancer conference. And when Aaron saunters into the room, still crisp but slightly disheveled in the handsomest way after attending conference sessions all day, I remember that somehow the universe booked us in the same room.

"Are you okay?" he asks, looking around my clothes strewn about the room. "It looks like a tornado stripped your clothes off."

And I wish it was you who stripped my clothes off.

Gosh darn it, brain—I may have admitted that I have feelings for Aaron, but that doesn't mean a whole lot just yet. I haven't even had time to process it. I've been sleeping.

"Was exhausted after a few sessions," I say, rubbing my eyes. "Needed to get some rest."

He sits on the lonely chair and sets down his briefcase, spreading his thick thighs and giving me a perfect view of his crotch. My chest tingles when I see a patch of sweat down there. He always got real sweaty, which embarrassed him, but I thought it was hot.

"Any luck finding a good cause?" he asks, folding his legs. Which is good because I was distracted by the view.

I shake my head. "Nada. You?"

He nods happily. "I think so. I met an investor from Manhattan who's willing to hear me out. We're gonna go get some dinner in a little bit to discuss potential next steps."

My chest sinks. But I don't know why. I should be happy for him. He's getting the funding he needs to make his research dreams come true. Yet the sinking feeling persists, and I can't help but feel like I've lost something, or I'm about to lose something. Is this 'something' Aaron?

"That's awesome, man," I say, pushing the sadness down. "I had a feeling you'd find someone quick."

He blushes, and my stomach flutters. I love seeing him happy.

I glance out the window. The summer sun hasn't set, but it's getting there. I check my watch to see that I was asleep for a good four hours.

"Man, I slept through the rest of today's sessions," I say, ruffling my hair.

"Sounds like you needed the rest," Aaron says, standing up. He takes off his suitcoat and sets it on the dresser, then starts undoing his tie. "I'm glad you got it."

There's that thoughtful Aaron. He was always like this in college, reminding me to physically take care of myself—eat right, sleep well, and so on. Which I needed as a rowdy football player at Miss U. But Aaron never minded. He was—how do they say it in the bible? Long-suffering. But I don't think he was suffering with me. I think he really enjoyed being around me.

But that still doesn't explain why he left.

"So you're going to meet this guy for dinner?" I ask. There's that sinking feeling again, and for some reason I feel like I'm being cheated on.

"Yeah," he says, starting to unbutton is shirt. "Gonna get into something more casual and head out in a bit."

As the sinking feeling remains, my post-nap brain fog clears enough for me to recognize where it's coming from. Aaron needs funding, and I'm somebody who can provide it. Sure, now that I've accepted I still like Aaron, I don't really *need* to find someone to fund now. But *he* needs it. So what's stopping me from helping him out?

Besides, seeing him seek someone else out to do it feels... really, like he is cheating on me. Like once he has someone, he has another opportunity to walk away from me. Because after that, when the conference is over, we have no real reason to keep in touch. And, more than anything, I want us to stay talking. To possibly see if we can try each other out again. Just one last try.

"Can I come with you?" I ask.

He turns to me with a furrowed brow, his shirt now open. And he isn't wearing an undershirt, so I can perfectly see just how muscular his torso has gotten over the years. Gosh, that's the perfect amount of beef and hair.

"To meet with this investor?" he asks, turning away when he sees me peaking. "You want to join us?"

My nerves overwhelm me, and I feel just like I did when I was waiting in line to talk to the woman who gave the breast cancer presentation: overwhelmed and unqualified.

"Yeah," I say shrugging. I rack my mind for a compelling excuse. And I find one that doesn't even feel like a lie.

"'Cause, you know, I've been having a hard time. I don't know how to approach some of these people to ask about their projects and if we'd be a good fit. Figured it'd be good to watch a pro do it."

His brow remains furrowed, then it relaxes. "Sure," he says. "Heard the restaurant we're going to is pretty nice as well."

The sinking feeling disappears, and I'm relieved. I don't want to go to sabotage his chance with the investor or anything. It's not like I really even want to pitch to fund his project either. At least not yet. Now that I know I like him, I just want to be with Aaron. And maybe, if it somehow works out, I can find a way to him in my life even after the conference, whether it's through funding or not.

"Great," I say, feeling a slight pain in my stomach. "Because I didn't eat lunch, and I'm starving."

Chapter 7

Aaron Watkins

As I PUT ON some fresh clothes in the privacy of the bathroom, I can't tell if the butterflies in my stomach are the result of excitement or fear.

Today was rough. After showing up late to my first session, I tried hard to get the attention of the investors there. But they were too busy trying to talk to the speaker. And with each passing session, I just grew more and more discouraged.

These other researchers had more resources and years in the academy, industry, and or even both, deftly summarizing their research, why it was important, and what funding they needed. But here I am just finishing my first year as a professor and struggling to find basic resources of my own.

Luckily, Laura was feeling good enough by lunchtime to meet up at a nearby restaurant. When I told her how they consolidated the room with someone else, she was on her knees—literally—apologizing to me. I had to reassure her multiple times that it wasn't her fault, and eventually she felt satisfied when I made her promise to watch *Rent* with me when I visit her for Thanksgiving this fall, which she hates but will put up with for me. But I didn't tell her who I am rooming with, or the fact that there is only one bed. Because that would mean confessing how I dated a man just before he joined the NFO and how I definitely might still have feelings for him, which I'm absolutely not ready to talk about.

But during our lunch date, Laura, as always, helped me feel more confident in myself as an academic. So confident that I walked straight up to an investor after the next session to see if he'd be interested in funding children's leukemia research. And after sharing with him my project details—which I was able to retrieve thanks to Dominic—he asked me out to dinner to get more details.

This is definitely where all the excitement is coming from.

The fear, however, comes from the fact that Dominic will be joining us.

I fucking kissed the man. And then I just ran away. It felt cruel to do, but what would have happened if I didn't? I would have torn his clothes off right there. And Lord knows how hard it would have been to walk away then. I did us both a favor.

So, I don't know why I agreed to let him come. With how kind he's been to me on this trip, I didn't see how I could say no. And I hate to admit that after all that he said to me this morning, I'd like to spend more time with him. But that's it. We'll have this dinner, and the rest of this conference we'll be at arm's length. Plus, he and I won't even be talking that much. I'll be talking to the investor.

Once I put my cologne on, I walk out of the bathroom in a casual navy button-up and slacks. By the dresser, Kyle's all dressed up, wearing a well-fitting green polo and tight slacks. God, he's a specimen. Thankfully it won't be us two tonight. Seeing how good he looks now, I dread knowing what could happen if we had dinner alone. He always knew how to take me out and schmooze me, even when our relationship was a secret.

"Ready?" I ask.

He makes a gesture of putting his key card in his wallet and his wallet in his pocket. "Ready as I'll ever be," he says.

Embarrassed, I grab my wallet from the nightstand and put it in my pocket. "Thanks for the reminder," I say. And we head out the door. Once we're in the street, I'm surprised to see so many pedestrians out.

"So where are we meeting him?" Dominic asks, speaking over the sound of traffic.

"This place called Nuvalon," I say, looking at my phone. "Only a couple blocks away. Walkable."

"Sheesh," he says, squeezing between two oncoming pedestrians. "Don't know how people live here. Way too crowded for my tastes."

"Same," I say. "I actually love how quiet Iowa City is. You like St. Louis?"

"Oh yeah," he says when we reach a crosswalk. "It's a city but it feels like a quaint small town. People are nice, and they're happy to finally have an NFO team again."

Still looking at my phone, I step forward, and strong hands grab my waist and yank me back just before a car barrels by and honks right where I would have stepped.

"Sorry," I say. "Thanks."

"You're good," he says, still holding my waist. "Just look where you're going."

And I blush as memories flood my mind. I remember walking home from the bars together after we went out with his friends. Of course, we told the others we were just friends, but we went home together all the same. And it was him, even when he was more drunk, making sure I didn't hurt myself or walk into traffic as I tend to do when I'm inebriated or preoccupied. I loved the way he took care of me. And it seems like this tendency of his hasn't gone away.

Finally, we can cross, and Dominic lets go of me. But I think both of us wanted him to keep his hands there.

Eventually, after crossing several streets—more carefully this time—we reach the restaurant. It's all dark and chic inside, the walls a deep maroon and the booths dark and plush. Tables are lit mostly by candlelight with dim lanterns above giving barely anymore light. A little too romantic for a meeting with an investor.

"Nice place," Dominic says, wiping a little sweat off his forehead.

"Two?" the hostess asks.

Dominic nods, but I shake my head. "Three," I say. I steal a glance at Dominic to see what that was about, but he's looking away.

She guides us to this isolated table toward the back with two chairs. Dominic and I sit across from each other, and she pulls up another chair to an empty spot at the table.

"Sorry," she says. "We typically have parties of two. I'll go grab a plate and more silverware."

And when she leaves, there's a tightening in my chest. The investor probably thought it would be just the two of us. Will Dominic being here ruin my chances at funding?

Dominic investigates the menu while I check my phone. It's three after seven, our agreed meeting time. I go ahead and shoot a text to Bill, the investor, and tell him I've arrived.

He responds immediately. "Walking in now," he says. And the tightening goes away.

"How about I order us an appetizer?" Dominic asks. "Crab cakes look great."

"Sure," I say. "I'm sure Bill will like it." I know this place is swanky and romantic, but this is not a date. This is a meeting with an investor. And that's what I'm trying to remind the both of us.

We both take a couple minutes looking over more of the menu, but then I realize that Bill should have arrived by now. I check my phone and don't see a message.

"What do you think you'll order?" Dominic asks.

And that's when I get an incoming call from Bill.

"One second," I say, stepping up and away from the table. I sequester myself in a dark, quiet corner of the restaurant and answer the call.

"Aaron here," I say.

"Yeah, Aaron," he says, and there's impatience in his voice. "Where are you?"

My chest tightens. I've already displeased him.

"I'm here," I say. "I got us a table in the back."

"I don't see you. I've asked the staff, and they say there's no Aaron here at all. Which location did you go to?"

My stomach sinks. "There are multiple locations?"

"Yeah. Are you at the one on 11th or 16th?"

My forehead breaks into a sweat. I can already feel this funding slipping beneath my fingers as I put my phone on speaker and open up my maps.

"11th," I say.

He sighs, and I swear I can see him rubbing his forehead in exasperation. "I'm at 16th," he says flatly. "Did you see my message about the location?"

"I'm so sorry," I say. "I must have mistyped it into my phone. I can rush over there now."

"No," he says. "It'll take you at least thirty to get here, and I don't have that much time."

It feels like I've been kicked in the gut.

"Let's reschedule," he says. "I might have some other time open this weekend." But he doesn't sound very enthusiastic about it. And I wouldn't either, not after getting practically stood up.

"Please forgive me," I say. "I'm open any time this weekend. I'll pay for dinner next time too. I really hope we get another chance. It already seems like we're a good fit."

"Yeah," he says, sounding distracted. "I have your number. I'll reach out later. Gotta go." And then he hangs up, and I'm feeling just as hopeless as I did when I was rushing back to my room this morning. I've just lost a funding opportunity.

I don't know how long it takes, but eventually I manage to make it back to the table. I plop down in my chair.

Dominic's already ordered us some water and my favorite cocktail, a Kentucky mule.

"You remembered," I say forlornly.

"Of course I did," he says, looking up from his menu. Then his face hardens. "You alright? What happened?"

Right. Because of course Dominic can still read me like a fucking picture book.

"He's not coming," I say. "The investor."

"What do you mean he's not coming?"

"We went to the wrong location. Apparently, we were supposed to go to the one on 16th street. This is 11th." I check my message history with Bill. "But he didn't even specify that in his message. How was I supposed to know that?"

"Oh man," Dominic says, setting down his menu. "I'm sorry. That really stinks."

I let out a sharp breath through my nose at his choice of words. He never likes to use the word 'suck'. Unless it's in the literal sense. Oh god, I cannot think about Dominic sucking anything right now.

"But you shouldn't be mad at yourself," he says. "Clearly this man didn't communicate that to you. That's on him."

I fold my arms. "Yeah, but I'm the one paying for it. Literally. I doubt he'll want to see me after this mess."

"Maybe you dodged a bullet," he says. "Because this shows that he'll probably be a frequently bad communicator if you work together. You wouldn't want such unreliable funding."

I huff out a breath. "Better than no having no funding at all."

The waiter comes to our table. "Have you two had a chance to look at the menu? I've also been told there will be a third. Are we still expecting them?"

Dominic looks at me. "You wanna stay?" he asks. "And don't worry—it's my treat."

"You don't have to do that," I say.

"Let me," he says, his eyes shining. "For old time's sake."

As Dominic and the waiter both rest their eyes on me, I shift in my seat and stare at the table, remembering all the lavish dinners Dominic took me out to in college. Now that the investor isn't coming—or rather that we aren't the ones coming to him—I don't see a point in staying.

But there's also no point in leaving, either. Dominic even wants to stay and pay for the whole thing just like he used to. And, come to think of it, I'm pretty hungry. This morning, after sleeping in Dominic's arms, I was still a bit too shocked to eat that much for breakfast, and I was so eager to catch up with Laura that I didn't eat much for lunch.

I know this means more alone time with Dominic, but we're already here, and I can go back to avoiding him after this is over.

So what the hell.

"They won't be joining," I say to the waiter, then look at Dominic. "Let's eat."

"Great," the water says, picking up the extra plate. "What can I get for you?"

And just before I respond, I swear I see a smile flash across Dominic's face.

Chapter 8

Dominic Johnson

I DON'T KNOW IF I believe in the same God that my parents taught me about, but I definitely sent a prayer of thanks to him after Aaron answered our waiter's question.

He and I are eating alone together. *It's a date.*

Aaron's still got that sad look in his eyes. I can tell he's blaming himself for what happened with this investor. But my goal for this dinner is to get him smiling ear to ear by the end. And I'm confident I can. I've done it before.

The waiter arrives with our crab cakes, and I insist he get first dibs. As I'm serving one for myself, he takes a bite, and then his eyes bug out.

"Oh my god," he says. "That's fucking delicious. Sorry."

I laugh. "You don't need to apologize for cussing. I'm glad you like it."

"Christ," he says, taking another bite. "This is good. I didn't realize how hungry I was."

"Then it's good we're eating. I know how you tend to skip meals when you get stressed. You definitely deserve to eat too."

His face reddens as he takes a sip of water. "Thanks," he says. "You're right."

"You always reminded me to eat," I say. "Just returning the favor."

We both scarf down our crabcakes in silence, and I'm trying to think of what I can say next. I want to him over to me in this conversation somehow—get him to really open up this time, then stay open instead of just running away.

He's looking down at his hand, going between pulling on his fingers and picking off the callouses.

"You still upset about what happened with the investor?"

He notices me looking at his hand—recognizing that I remember his nervous habit—and relaxes. "I mean, yeah. That was my one successful lead today. And I just ruined it by going to the wrong restaurant."

"But you have the rest of the weekend. It could still work with him, or you could find someone else."

He sighs and leans back. "But what if this was the only opportunity I can possibly get? And I just ruined it all?"

I lean forward and rest my elbows on the table. "You remember when you failed that O Chem exam your junior year?"

He lets out a sharp laugh and nods. "Like it was yesterday."

"You came over to my apartment almost balling your eyes out, thinking they were going to revoke your scholarship and send you back home. Heck, you practically thought you were going to prison."

"Because those things could have happened! Well, the scholarship thing could have."

"But did it?" I ask.

He sighs and shakes his head. "No."

"What happened instead?"

"I wasn't the only one who failed," he says. "Well, there wasn't anyone who didn't fail. In fact, I got one of the highest grades."

"And then you got to retake it, along with everyone else."

He nods slowly.

"You're so quick to catastrophize, man. Like something bad happens and then you think it's the end of the world. You don't need to do that to yourself. I know you don't believe in God, but trust something to get you through. You gotta let some things be."

"But if I try to relax, I might miss an opportunity I would have otherwise seen if I was on high alert." He wipes his mouth with his napkin and pushes out his chair. "I should leave and go back to the hotel. Maybe I can find someone there."

Before he can stand up, I reach over the table and hold his hand. He looks up at me with wide eyes. This is the first time we've touched skin-to-skin since the kiss.

"Aaron, you can stand to relax and eat," I say. "Take care of yourself first. Then let the rest sort itself out. I promise it will."

He stares at me with rigid shoulders, then relaxes. "You really think something will work out?"

I nod. "Of course I do. Especially for you. There's no one I know more qualified. And I've seen a lot of presentations. Knowing you, I'd choose to fund you over any one of them."

And I mean every word.

He squeezes my hand, then lets it go as he scooches himself back into the table.

And then our food arrives. After some insistence, I got Aaron to order the lobster he had been eyeing on the menu. I'm paying, after all. And I ordered the lamb with caramelized vegetables and potatoes. Once the waiter's gone, we dig in.

Aaron audibly moans, making me stir below. "I can't remember the last time I've had anything this tasty," he says.

"Me either, honestly," I say, eating my lamb faster than I'd like to admit.

"I feel like I've talked a lot about myself," he says. "How you been all these years?"

My mind immediately goes to all my efforts to get a woman. I can still hear the mean laugh of the girlfriend who mocked me for not being able to stay hard while having sex with her. And how after it seemed like I could never get a woman to stick around me. Which spurred me to go on this ridiculous journey in the first place. I wanted to bolster my image so I could actually get a girl to both want me *and* stay in a relationship with me.

But things are different now. After all, reflecting on my feelings for Aaron, I know I really like men—specifically this man. And this realization explains why

I could never keep a woman around. It's like they subconsciously picked up that I liked men, so they knew I just couldn't be interested in them. Which is why they always left me. It wasn't personal—it was just my sexuality. And that makes perfect sense.

But Aaron doesn't need to know all this. So, I keep the conversation focused on us.

"Been missing you a lot," I say truthfully. "Every time I see a musical I think of you."

He perks up. "You're... watching musicals?"

I give the most humble shrug I can. "Every now and then. You got me really into Les Mis."

He puts on the most genuine smile I've seen on him this trip, and it makes me grin.

"What?" I ask.

"You're telling me that a man in the NFO for six years is secretly watching musicals?" He laughs. "I don't believe you," he says, more jokingly than seriously.

"You know what musical I've been dying to see?" I ask.

"Uh, obviously," he says, scooping up some lobster and rice.

"The Book of Mormon."

His jaw drops, and his handsome face makes my whole body thrum. Just as I wanted, his enthusiastic self is returning. The man I used to know and love.

"You mean the 'Turn it off, like a light switch' Book of Mormon musical?"

I furrow my brow. "I don't know the music, but I've heard it's hilarious."

He shakes his head and looks at me like he knows something I don't. "You don't know the half of it."

"Maybe we could see it together."

"Dominic Johnson," he says, grinning. "Are you asking me on a date?"

My face goes red. "And if I am?"

He sighs, almost deflating, his face getting serious. And as silence comes over us, I feel the mood of the conversation turn.

"You're asking me after all that happened between us?"

My stomach sinks. I wanted to have this conversation, but I wasn't expecting it to happen now. Especially when everything was going so well.

Whatever. Better now than never.

"You did hurt me," I admit. "A lot."

He leans forward and rubs the bridge of his nose. "I know."

"The least you could do was give me some closure," I say. "Instead of just saying 'it can't work' and then ghosting me."

"I know," he says, rubbing his forehead now, seemingly more annoyed with himself than me.

"It's just—" He grunts and leans his head back, then whips it forward. "What else was I supposed to do? Your career in the NFO was about to take off. It was a matter of time."

"How?" I say, my hurt showing in my voice. "How on earth was it a matter of time?"

"What gay and out players do you know in the NFO?" he asks.

I think about Kyle Weaver and the other guys I fooled around with after Aaron on the Miss U football team, but we had an agreement that we'd keep each other a secret.

But that's exactly Aaron's point. There are no out players.

"So you didn't even want to give us a try?" I ask.

He drops his face into his hands and rubs his face. "We did try us, Dominic. And it was great. But it wouldn't have stayed great with you in the NFO. Too many hurdles and too much stigma toward gay people. Which is why I had to do what I did. Staying with you then would have only made the inevitable breakup harder in the future."

"Sheesh, Aaron," I say. "I'm not your parents. I wasn't going to walk out on you like they did."

He whips up his head, his face pure anger. "You can't say that. You don't know what you would have done if we stayed together. I was protecting both of us from getting hurt." He exhales through his nose. "I was protecting myself."

I sit there, my chest heaving, as the anger gradually leaves his face. But neither of us say anything. We just stew in all the words we threw at each other.

"You're right," I say. "I don't know what could have happened."

He folds his arms and stares at the table as I speak, but I can tell he's listening.

"But that's true for anything. So why don't we give it another try? You and me?"

His brow forms a V as he looks up at me. "You're serious?" But his voice isn't dead or skeptical. There's hope there.

"As a heart attack," I say. "I know I'm in the NFO, but we can make something work. We can keep it hidden until we don't have to. It's just—seeing you on this trip, hearing your voice, sleeping in the same bed, *kissing you*—"

He blushes and looks down.

"It's all made me see that I miss you. I miss you so fucking much."

"Dominic!"

I put my hand up. "I use the word 'cause I mean it," I say. "Please, Aaron. Don't run away from me again. I want to give this another try. See where we can go."

He studies my face, chewing on his lips, and this feels more intimate than most things we've ever done. His brown eyes search mine, and I'm tempted to squirm and hide under the table. But I resist the urge. Because I want this. I want him.

"And I know this could be a conflict of interest, but I mean it when I say that I could fund you. I don't know all the logistics of your project, but that could be ironed out. I have the people hired who could help, and I have money to give. And that's what you need."

He chews on his lips harder, the gears in his brain going. Then he leans forward, and my stomach does a little jump. Here's his answer.

"I've missed you too," he says.

And it feels like fireworks are going off in my torso.

"I have my fears," he says. "But you're right. Maybe I did run away too soon. Maybe we could work out with you still in the NFO. And honestly, I would be lying if I didn't say I had regrets about leaving you. So..."

He trails off, and I lean forward.

"So what?" I ask.

"I think we can try again," he says.

The fireworks spread throughout my entire body, and I can't help but smile as I lean back in my chair.

"Alright," I say. "Perfect."

The waiter comes with the check, and before I know it, we're back on the streets of New York City. To get an early start to the day tomorrow, we both decide to make our way back to the hotel.

"Give me some time to think about funding together," Aaron says. "I also want to see what other options I have."

"Of course," I say, relieved that Aaron's even accepted giving our relationship another go. It feels like a dream. "Take your time."

As we walk, Aaron extends his hands to hold mine, but they're deep in my pockets. And I don't take them out.

Back in college, we knew the drill. In private, we could be as intimate as we liked. But in public, we could only be friends. We both knew it had to be this way for me to have any promising career in the NFO. But that didn't mean it didn't hurt.

And it especially hurts that I can't be affectionate with him now. Even as he's giving me another chance.

"Can I ask you something?" Aaron asks as we walk.

"Of course," I say, watching the sidewalk, hands still deep in my pockets.

"You remember that time you came home from that game versus Alabama?"

My blood runs cold, but I nod. "Sure do."

"You were pissed," he says. "And not just because you lost."

My heart starts to race as I recall the memory. "Yeah, you're right."

I expect him to retell the memory, but he doesn't. He says nothing, as if waiting for me to tell it. So I decide to take the bait.

"The guys on the other team," I say. "Caught rumor about things going on at Miss U. That entire game, they ran around the field calling us all sorts of slurs. Getting in our heads."

"And when you came home, you were shaken. You weren't yourself for days."

I nod, my shoulders already tightened from this conversation.

Because that's what I hate more than anything else. It wasn't that I couldn't get hard for that girl. It was how she treated me for not being able to. Like I was some piece of garbage. That's how those guys on that field made me feel: disgusting, worthless.

I can accept that I'm gay. But I don't know if I can accept the shame that so often comes with it.

"Is this going to happen again?"

I look at him as we stop at a crosswalk, only a block away from our hotel. "What do you mean?"

"When you shut down after that, it was hard for me. I thought *you* were going to be the one to break up with me. I wished you had just told me what was going through your head. I know now that that's what I need in a relationship. I need you to communicate with me. So, can I expect that? Or should this just end now before it starts?"

We start walking again, and I chew on my lips.

"Give me a minute to think."

We reach the hotel and silently make our way to the elevator. Once we reach our floor, we slowly walk to our door.

Truthfully, I never opened up to Aaron about it because I was worried he would think I'm disgusting for even having these thoughts about myself. But that's clearly not true. In fact, he's saying he wants to know what's going on inside me.

Out of anyone I've ever known, Aaron has been the most truthful, genuine, and kind. And now he's willing to try again with me one last time. He wants me to be open and honest. I don't know what I can do about the shame that comes with being gay, but I can do anything that Aaron asks of me. In fact, I will do anything.

Once we're inside our room, I put my hands on Aaron's shoulders and rub his neck with my thumbs.

"I will be as open as I possibly can," I say. "That you can expect of me."

He melts into my touch, and my hands are tempted to search and rediscover his entire body. It's amazing what the body can remember when it feels something familiar.

"Then I'm ready," he says.

And so begins our second try.

I press my forehead against his, our lips only an inch away. "Do I have the permission to make love with you?" I ask. "It's been a while, so I know I'm clean."

He runs his hands up my shirt, sending warm shivers down my spine.

"Same," he says. "And you absolutely do."

Chapter 9

Aaron Watkins

WHEN OUR LIPS TOUCH for the second time, my entire body jolts to life.

Dominic Johnson and I are for real. Again.

As we kiss, my mind reels. This was the last thing I thought could happen. But after hearing how willing he is to really try this out, I would be a fool to let him go. Because seeing him again awakened in me the grief about our relationship that I had buried for so many years. And now, I'm confident that Aaron won't run away from me like I was afraid of. There are still things to work out, such as his NFO career and his feelings about his sexuality, but with his willingness, these don't seem so insurmountable now.

He releases his hold from my mouth and starts kissing across my cheek and down my neck. Each peck is like a tiny explosion of pleasure.

He raises himself to my ear. "I'm gonna make you feel so good, Aaron Watkins."

Chills.

"Have you—" I pause. I don't really know how to ask this.

"Have I... been busy?" he asks for me. The backs of his hands are rubbing up and down my button-up. With anyone else, I would feel embarrassed having them caress the part of my body I'm most insecure about. But I like Dominic touching me here.

"Yeah," I say, laughing from embarrassment.

He plants gossamer kisses across my cheek, then forehead. Already, he's traversing my body with a finesse that proves he's been busy since he's last seen me. Which is okay, of course. I wouldn't expect him not to. It's just the thought of him with someone else makes me want to vomit up the lobster I just ate.

He grabs my chin and points my face up to his. "I slept with a few other guys after you in college. And some women. But they all pale in comparison to you."

I laugh at that as I remove his hand from my chin. With how hot and earnest Dominic is, I doubt I'm the best person he's ever slept with.

"Right. Because the person you lose your virginity to is always the best sexual experience ever," I say.

That's when Dominic grabs hold of my ass and lifts me up against him. Startled, I wrap my arms around the back of his neck. Then he gently sets me down on the bed, my legs propped up behind him by the shelf of his ass. I fall on my back, and he starts unbuttoning my shirt.

When my shirt is completely open and has my hands pinned down on either side of me. I'm tempted to cover up my hairy belly, but I couldn't even if I wanted to. And I don't. Because Dominic's eyeing me the same way he eyed his lamb. God, he still looks at me like I'm the sexiest thing to walk the planet.

"With you, it's not just sex," he says. "It's love. You know that."

I swallow, surprised. Years ago, sex between us was mostly me fucking and pleasing him. In other words, I took charge. We both enjoyed it, don't get me wrong. But I've never seen him this aggressive.

And I like it.

"And if you don't believe you're not the best I've ever had, fine," he says. "You can try to prove me wrong if you want. But I doubt I am."

Grinning, I try to push him off me. But he doesn't budge. I know he's in the NFO, but goddamn this guy is strong.

In a swift movement, he grabs my legs and pulls me to the edge of the bed. He puts my legs around him, then runs his hands through my belly and chest hair. Even through both our pants, I can feel just how hard he is.

"I'm gonna show you how much you've been missing over the years," he says.

As his thumbs draw circles around my nipples and his dick puts just enough pressure on my hole, I believe him. This is more way more advanced than what we did.

"You're gonna top me?"

He nods, then shrugs. "If you'll let me."

He thrusts hard into me, and I can't help but moan.

"Seems like you want it," he says.

I bite my lip. Of course, Dominic's ass is wonderful, but I'd be silly to turn down the offer to be topped by a beautiful man.

"I do," I say. "Let me clean up down there before we start though."

He leans over and plants a soft kiss on my lips. "Of course."

He pulls off me, and I make my way to my carry-on to grab my bulb and lube that I decided to bring on a whim in case I somehow got action. And thank God I did bring this stuff. Because the thought of missing out on Dominic topping me fills me with poignant dread.

"Don't undress yet," I say just as he's grabbed hold of the collar of his shirt. "Wait for me to do that."

I toss him the lube, and he releases his collar to catch it with a grin.

"See you soon," he says, his voice low. And I practically tingle from head to toe.

I shut the bathroom door behind me with a sigh that could speak volumes. As I clean myself up, I really think over what I'm doing. I'm effectively agreeing to start a relationship with Dominic Johnson. But I could end things now. I could save myself a lot of hurt if I just walked away. That way I can eliminate the possibility of him abandoning me for good.

Or I could just take a risk. I could just see this through.

I've missed the man like crazy, and I've held myself back from so many other potential partners out of fear that they would leave me just like I feared he would. Just like my parents did.

Dominic mentioned that I deserve to treat myself kindly by feeding myself and taking it easy. I think I also deserve to treat myself to a relationship. Even if it might not work out.

So I think I will.

Once I'm all cleaned up, I come back into the room, my slacks back on with my shirt unbuttoned. Dominic's laying on the bed reading, taking up all the space with his giant, muscled body. But when he sees me, he sets down the book and gestures for me to join him.

And I do so happily.

I straddle him, loving his lips with mine. My tongue digs into his mouth, and there's a faint taste of mint from the candy they gave us after dinner. But the rest tastes like him. Feral now, I kiss him harder, bucking my ass back onto his hard dick. I try to pin his arms down, but he grabs my wrist before I can even get a good grip. And then he gives me the most sickening grin.

"Oh no you don't," he says.

Before I can even tell what's happened, he has me flipped onto his back. My legs are spread around him, and he's got my hands pinned above my head.

"I'll tell you how this is going to go," he says, almost growling.

I let out a whimper and nod, my entire body electrified.

He lowers to kiss my shoulder. Then he does the unimaginable. He sticks his tongue out and licks all the way to my ear. My entire body convulses, but my resistance is useless against him. Which makes it so much better.

"Since it's been a while," he says. "You're gonna tell me what you like. What you want me to do to you. And then you're gonna let me take my time pleasing you." His tongue searches inside my ear, and I nearly squeal with pleasure. He pulls out just as I'm about to beg for more. "You're gonna make up for all the years you left me hanging. Do you understand?"

"Yes."

"Say my name when you talk to me," he says. "I want to hear my name on your lips."

"Yes, Dominic," I say obediently.

He groans with pleasure, then raises up to look me in the eyes. His blue eyes pierce mine, and the scent of his leathery cologne mixed with the sweat he's worked up all day has me breathing rapidly so I take it all in. He's got fresh blonde stubble because he hasn't shaved today, and his strawberry blonde hair is perfectly disheveled.

"So tell me," he says. "What do you want?"

With his dick pressing so hard against me, it's hard to think straight. But I manage.

"Taking charge like this," I say. "A hard yes."

"Alright," he says. "Anything else?"

It's been a while since I've had any good sex, so I think back over the years. Whenever I've bottomed, I've always liked to forgo my climax until the top has gotten completely off. Something about that deference really gets me. I like to stroke myself while letting the top use me too—to edge—but I haven't done it all that often. I'm not sure why.

"When I bottom, I'm tempted to cum quickly. But don't let me. Keep me going for a while. And don't let me cum until you say."

He chuckles. "Easy."

"And that's it," I say. "Have at me."

He leans down and presses his lips against mine with the most passionate kiss yet. He eyes me hungrily as he pulls away. "Take your clothes off," he commands.

He releases his hold on my hands, and I quickly sit up to shimmy my shirt off. Then I slide off the bed to pull my slacks off all while he patiently watches me. When I take my boxers off, my dick bounces up from the waistband, and Dominic smirks.

"Happy to see me," he says. He then gets up from the bed and stands up right in front of me. "Now undress me."

I start with his shirt. I grab the bottom, and he raises his arms in the air as I pull it off him. His round pecs lower with his arms, and I can't help but reach up and fondle them. He flexes, and I laugh.

"Gotten bigger, haven't I?"

I roll my eyes as I feel his biceps. "And cockier." Jesus, his arms are sturdy.

"That's big too," he says with a boyish smile. "But of course you already know that."

I can't wipe the grin off my face. "Don't make me regret this."

"You won't once you take my pants off," he says.

And when I do, he's right. His eight-inch dick curves up to me, and I swear I can see his veins pulsating. This man is this hard. *For me.* I can't believe he *still* wants me. Even after all these years.

"Sit down on the bed," he says gently.

I obey, trying not to notice the way the fat of my body moves.

"You are so beautiful," Dominic says, stroking my cheek as his dick pokes against my chest. "I hope you know that."

"I guess," I say shyly.

He grabs my chin and lifts my face to him again. "You are," he says. "You got the body of a real man. And I mean, look at this." He points to his dick.

I laugh. "Yeah, yeah. You're right."

"Trust me when I say I want to be with you." He gestures to me. "This is the 'you' I want to be with."

I blush. "Well thank you," I say. I marvel at his muscular, beefy body. "You're beautiful too."

He flexes his biceps again. "I know."

I roll my eyes and laugh. "And so vain." But I'm not really complaining. Because the bragging makes him so much hotter. Already salivating and feeling completely comfortable in my body, I lean down to suck him, but he stops me with his hand.

"Listen carefully," he says. "First, put your mouth on it. And then go as deep as you can. If any of this is too much, either tap me three times on the leg or say Les Mis."

I nod.

"My name, Aaron."

"Yes, Dominic," I say, his command sending warm chills right down to my dick. So, he's a dom and an expert in consent now? Damn. I'll do anything he tells me.

I lower and cover the head of his dick with my mouth. He lets out a moan, and I feel proud for pleasing him. I swirl my tongue around the head, taking in the sweat and precum that's accumulated, then go further.

He stops me again.

My mouth still around him, I look up, confused.

"You take your time when you're enjoying me," he says. "Show me with your tongue how much you're enjoying it, then you can go further."

I nod, then use my tongue to create a small pocket of suction under his dick. When he moans, I know I'm doing what he wants. I steadily lap my tongue against it, creating more suction with my cheeks, and his knees falter a bit.

"Gosh, man," he says. "Just like that. Now go deeper."

I keep up the same motions as I slide further down his dick, and Dominic's huge body convulses under my tongue.

"As far as you can go," he says.

I keep going until my eyes water and his strawberry blonde pubes tickle my nose, the only air I'm getting the musk from his crotch. This is when I notice how hard I am.

"Now I want you stroke yourself," he says. "But only use your own spit from my dick as lube."

I release my lips from his dick momentarily, and a glob of spittle threatens to drip onto the floor. I grab it with my hands and use it as lube to stroke myself just as I put my lips around his cock again.

But it feels weird.

Not the sucking, of course, but stroking myself. When I've submitted in the past, guys didn't care what I did while I pleased them, and they definitely didn't tell me to stroke myself. Edging while I'm getting Dominic off almost feels too... indulgent.

"Good boy," he says. "Don't stop until I say. But don't you dare think of cumming."

I nod, barely able with his whole dick in my mouth.

Good boy. We never said anything like this in college, and it's definitely encouraging me to keep stroking. Whoever he slept with after me to get this experience deserves some kudos. Because this is fucking hot.

Now, I'm going up and down his dick, keeping up the tongue action. I've made Dominic's knees so weak that now he's got one leg propped up on the bed. But that only gives me a better view of his thick, furry thighs. So I'm not complaining.

"God, you are amazing, Aaron Watkins," he says, now thrusting himself in and out of my mouth.

Encouraged by his enthusiasm, I stroke myself faster as he uses me, feeling close already.

"Alright," he says, stepping away, pulling his dick out of my mouth.

I wipe spit from my face and immediately stop stroking myself.

He gently grabs my chin and forces me to look up at him. "I didn't tell you to stop masturbating."

"Yes, Dominic," I say. And I get back to it.

"Good boy. Now get on the bed," he says. "Lay on your back. Spread your legs."

I obey, and he puts himself right between me. He leans over me to get his balance, his arms on either side of my head. Without thinking, I raise my head and use my tongue to put his entire nipple in my mouth.

"Oh," he says, his body tensing. "Yes, do that."

He reaches over to the nightstand to grab the lube as I suck on his nipple. With my lips, I hold his pec in place, using my tongue to lap up his hairy nipple. And it feels like I've been possessed. I taste the mixture of his salty sweat and skin, and I'm insatiable. I lick and suck harder, as if in doing so I can swallow him whole and carry him inside me wherever I go. I never really knew this until now, but I think I'm a mouth guy. I want to do more sexual things with my mouth.

"Easy," he says, pulling away. "You're gonna get me to cum this way."

I smirk up at him. "Like that could be so bad."

"Don't disobey me," he says with a smile. He squirts lube onto his hand. "Or else."

"Oh really?" I ask. "Or else what?"

He presses his thick, lubed thumb against my hole—just presses—and I gasp.

"Or I'll remind you who's really in charge." He presses harder, and I grasp the bed sheets.

He chuckles. "Aaron Watkins. If I had known you were this easy to control, I would have done this to you every day."

"Well we can start the streak now," I say.

"Dang right."

He uses his pinky to open me up, which is still a lot considering how beefy his hands are. Then he moves to his middle finger, then two at a time. I stop pleasing myself and hold my knees so I can concentrate on him opening me up.

"I didn't tell you to stop, Aaron," he says, removing his fingers from me. "You'll open up easier if you stroke yourself."

"Sorry," I say, grabbing my dick again. "It's just that I'm not used to getting myself off while being so submissive."

He leans over, his arms on either side of me. "Les Mis—let's talk. In my experience, I know some guys just like to focus on the sensation of bottoming during sex rather than masturbate along with it. Is that what you're saying?"

I pause for minute, then shake my head. "No, I love stroking myself while bottoming. I just don't think I've ever felt like I could. Like it would distract the top or something."

"When you said you wanted me to hold you back, I thought that's what you were referring to—edging, that is. That's why I've been telling you to keep stroking even when it's hard. Did I misunderstand you?"

My stomach leaps for some reason. "No, no. That's exactly what I meant. I just—sometimes, it's hard for me to say what I want, I guess."

I wince, afraid he'll want to probe into this deeper. But he just runs his hands through my hair like he used to, sending warmth down my spine.

"Do you want me to help edge you?" he asks.

I bite my lip, then take a deep breath. And I nod.

"Then we'll do it the way I like," he says. "Assuming you still want me in control?"

I nod, more emphatically this time.

He smirks. "Good. Now stroke yourself."

His words send what feels like a warm wave through my body. I start rubbing myself, slowly though so I don't cum before he says I can.

"There we go," he says. He caresses my cheek in a way that feels more tender than dominant, and I'm tempted to shove his whole thumb in my mouth. Which feels a little too wild for me.

"But I have to go slow," I say. "Or else I'll cum too early."

He chuckles. "You jerk off when I tell you and how fast I tell you. But you better pray if you cum too early."

I almost scoff as I laugh. "Dominic Johnson."

"You said you wanted me to take charge and edge you." He kisses my knee. "This is it."

I bite my lip, another way of chills coming over me. "Fine. But you're a dick."

"You can complain all you want," he says. "But you gotta obey me or you'll have to pay. I'll let you stroke slowly for now, how about that?"

"So merciful," I say sarcastically, moving my hand up and down my shaft deadly slow. He presses three fingers inside, and I nearly yelp.

After he removes them, he rubs the head of his dick against my hole. "You ready for this?"

I nod eagerly. "Dominic, please put it in me."

"Keep stroking and I will," he says. "Or else you go back to sucking."

"God, you're torture," I say, trying to push myself onto his dick.

"No," he says. "I'm your heaven."

I have to bite my lip to contain myself at that. And as he slowly slides in his lubed dick, gradually opening me up, I realize he's right. Because only heaven could feel this good.

I don't how I could have ever thought that Dominic would leave me. Look at how tenderly he's treating me, even using his own safe phrase to talk to me about my concerns. And he doesn't think I'm too fat or hairy—it's like I'm perfect with him. With how much he's into me, I'm the last person he would abandon. He's nothing like my parents. I'm safe with him. I'm finally safe.

Once he's all the way inside, both of us sing a duet with our moans.

"Oh, Lord," Dominic says. "Help me."

I chuckle, needing to take deep breaths to handle all of him inside me. "Not often you take the Lord's name in vain."

"Only when I need to," he says with a sigh. "Jesus, you're perfect."

"Dominic!"

"God, you're perfect," he says with emphasis, slowly pulling out. Once he's all the way out, he pushes it back inside slowly.

I whimper, stroking myself obediently. "I don't know how I'm gonna last."

"You're gonna last until I tell you to," he growls. "Stroke faster."

I obey as he pulls out, then let out a deep moan as he thrusts inside me again. Knowing I can't stop or even go any slower, I take deep, heavy breaths, focusing on holding myself back. It's torture, the sensation of holding back my orgasm white hot, but the pleasure is just as exquisite.

He leans over me and starts thrusting faster now. "I never knew you could feel this good."

And now he's hitting my prostate. I clutch the bed sheets with my free hand and shut my eyes, using all my strength to prevent myself from disobeying Dominic.

"Don't close your eyes," he says. "I want to you to watch me."

I open them wide and take in the beautiful man fucking me silly. His blue eyes shine with hunger as he bites his tongue, thrusting in and out of me. His muscular chest and belly bounce with each thrust, and his huge arms flex holding my legs in place.

"This isn't fair," I say as he fucks me. "You're too hot. You expect me to hold it in as I watch you plow me?"

"Not my problem," he says. "Do as I say."

Fuck.

I do my best to hold it in, but his concentrated, sweaty face somehow makes him look even hotter. Is this what he looks like on the football field? Christ.

It's like everyone of my nerves is on fire from the way he's fucking me, talking to me, controlling me. The only way for me not to cum now is to stare into his blue eyes and count each of his strokes to myself. And of course the pleasure is so good I keep losing count.

With anyone else, looking at him like this would feel weird. Too personal. But Dominic is like an old, loved t-shirt. I can slip him on with ease, so looking into his eyes is no different looking at a beautiful tree or captivating sunset. It's easy. God, how could I forget how easy this is?

Pretty soon, his face contorts, and I can tell he's trying hard not to cum.

"How do you feel so good?" he asks. He thrusts harder and faster, and I've gotten used to his size by now. I can take it. For a brief moment, it feels like I'm in charge. And I take advantage of it.

"Cum inside me, Dominic," I say. "Breed me for the first time just like I did you so many years ago."

"Oh my God," he says, taking the Lord's name in vain again. "God, Aaron, you're so—"

He lets out a guttural moan has he thrusts inside me so hard my head grazes the headboard. But I'm unphased. He pants over me, his entire body covered in sweat. With my free hand, I reach up and gently rub his nipples, trying to make his comedown as pleasurable as possible. I wrap my legs around him and pull him even deeper into me, feeling his huge, gorgeous ass with the heels of my feet. I squeeze my hole so I can carry every last drop of him with me.

He collapses into me and wraps his arms around my head, and I wipe my face all over his hairy, sweaty chest, taking in his pure man scent. My cock throbs in my hand, and I still don't even know how I've made it last this long without exploding. Dominic raises up, and we gaze into each other's eyes. I feel his cock slowly soften inside me, and I get the immediate urge to put it in my mouth and suck up any of the leftover cum. Which is gross. Because it's just been in my ass, and Dominic might think I'm weird for being so desperate.

"What's up?" he asks, running his hand through my hair again. "Your mind looks busy."

I want to ask if he can shove his cock so far down my throat it reaches my stomach, but I stop myself.

"You know," I say, pressing my cock into his hairy belly. "Just waiting to be released from this prison you put me in."

But he doesn't get up. In fact, he relaxes his weight into me, sandwiching my dick between our hairy bellies. If my hand wasn't wrapped around it, I fear this movement alone would send me over the edge.

"We can fix that," he says. He pecks me on the lips, thrusting gently into me. His stomach grazes against my hand covering my dick, and my stomach leaps. Feeling this friction against my dick, paired with his semi-hard dick still inside me, could be enough to scramble my brain.

"Tell me what you want, Aaron, and you'll get it," he says.

But I keep thinking about him straddling my face, his cock so deep in my throat I have to inhale his crotch sweat. God, I'm a fucking pervert. When his belly grazes the hand around my cock, I'm convinced that this will be a more acceptable way to cum.

"This position," I say. "Is perfect."

Without missing a beat, Dominic reaches between us and gently removes my hand from my dick. Then he nuzzles his hairy belly even harder onto me, completely encasing my dick between the two of us. I adjust myself against him and let out a groan from how good it makes my dick feel.

"Yeah," he says. "That's hot. Hump my belly with me inside you."

I obey eagerly. Each time I thrust my pelvis, I both rub myself against him and fuck myself on his cock, our sweat acting as my lube. My entire groin is hot with pleasure, and I know my climax will be explosive.

That's when Dominic leans down to make out with me, and I move my pelvis even faster. It doesn't take me long to reach the point of no-return. He pulls away and looks at me like I'm the most beautiful thing on this planet, and I return his gaze imploringly, asking him a question with my eyes alone.

"Yeah," he says, running his hand through my hair casually, as if I'm not using all my strength to hump his muscular body and fuck myself on his gorgeous dick. "Say my name as you cum for me."

And that sends me over the edge.

"Dominic," I moan, my face contorting in pleasure as my cum shoots in between us, still thrusting into him hungrily. "Dominic, Dominic, Dominic."

"That's it, Aaron," he says. "Good boy. There we go." He peppers my face with kisses while I chant his name quietly, my climax enduring.

As I come down, saying Dominic's name one last time, I forget how powerful edging is and how much I've missed doing it. Dominic is a saint and a soldier for pulling this dormant desire out of me. And for satisfying it perfectly.

Once my climax is over, I stop thrusting, but my body still convulses. Gradually, Dominic pulls himself out of me and before I know it, he's laying right next to me, wiping us both off with a towel. After we're clean, he takes me in his arms and squeezes me, and now I seriously feel that I've died and gone to heaven. Because there's truly no other explanation for how much joy I feel right now.

"How was that?" he asks.

"Do I even need to say?"

He laughs. "It was amazing for me too," he says.

And that's how the night ends. He helps me under the covers, then gets in behind me and wraps his arms around me just like the night before. And I fall asleep the happiest I've felt in a very long time.

Chapter 10

Dominic Johnson

When I wake up with Aaron Watkins in my arms, I'm afraid I'll get second thoughts. That I'll go back to thinking of all this as a phase and want to run away from Aaron just like he did me. But as I take in a deep breath of his skin where his back meets his neck, taking in his sweet, musky scent, I feel just as strongly as I did the night before.

Eventually, I get up while he's still asleep and start getting ready for the day. I smile at him as he stretches himself awake.

"Sleep well?" I ask.

"Better than ever," he says, getting comfortable again.

We both sit there for a minute, processing everything.

That was, hands-down, the best sex I've ever had. And it felt so right holding Aaron against me for the second time.

"How you feeling?" I ask, leaning against the dresser in some basketball shorts. "About us?"

He sighs. "I feel good," he says, clearly checking my shirtless body out. "Not sure how else I'm supposed to feel. But I'm really ready to give us a good shot."

My chest warms at that. "Good."

He rubs his eyes and makes his way to sitting up. "Are there any sessions you're planning to attend today?"

"Actually," I say, pushing myself off the dresser. I come and sit right next to him on the bed. He rubs my arm, then kisses it. And I kiss him.

"What?" he asks, massaging my arm.

"I figured at breakfast we could discuss logistics for how I would fund you," I say. "I know you still want to see what other options you may have. But it can't hurt."

He perks up. "So you're really willing to fund me?"

I almost laugh. "What? Did you think I was joking?"

"No," he says, shaking his head. "This is all just too much to believe. Getting back together with my ex who I still have feelings for *and* finding funding? It's too perfect."

I can't help but smile hearing his confession about his feelings for me. I lean in to kiss him. "Don't worry," I say. "I am really willing." I push up from the bed. "I'll get ready and go get some breakfast. I'm starving. I can pick up some for you, and then we can discuss during the first session. How's that sound?"

"Great," he says, leaning back against the headboard, his hairy, muscled, masculine body the picture of perfect.

Aaron lays down to get a little more rest while I shower and put my clothes on. As I walk out the door, I tell him I'll see him soon and say quick prayer of gratitude to God that He's put all this together. I continue that prayer all the way down to the main conference room.

I may not be super religious now, but I believe in God. And I believe He loves straight and gay people all the same. Now that I know I'm not really straight, I'm a little uncomfortable with the implications and what this means for my career and feelings toward women, but at the very least I know I'm loved no matter what kinda man I am.

Just outside the big conference room, I spot Kyle Weaver, the other NFO player who was part of the underground gay group at Miss U, talking with some beautiful girl. She's looking at him all stary-eyed, and I can tell he's putting on that modest, sweet talk I saw him do back at Miss U that could make any girl fall in love with him.

And suddenly I'm jealous.

No girl has ever looked at me like that. Now, I could chalk that up to the fact that I really do like men. That's what I realized on my date with Aaron, after all—that women could just pick up that I was gay, so they'd leave me.

But that doesn't make sense with Kyle Weaver. As far as I know, he likes men as much as I do. Yet women are crawling all over him like they're ants and he's honey. That means that my gay sexuality can't explain why women won't go after me. Kyle breaks that theory. So if it's not that, then… it has to be me. Something has to be wrong with me. There's something fundamentally broken inside me that keeps pushing women away.

Uneased by this realization, I go through the buffet line and get me and Aaron some breakfast. When I sit down and start eating, I try to think about how excited I am now that Aaron and I are sorta dating now. But all I can think about is how that doesn't matter because I'm still too flawed to get a girl.

Someone taps me on the shoulder. I turn to see the same beautiful redheaded woman who I tried to talk to back in the lobby when I first arrived. At that time, she didn't give me the time of day. But now she's staring at me the way I've seen Aaron stare at me when I'm shirtless.

"Are you Dominic Johnson?" she asks.

"Sure am," I say, turning to her.

"The NFO player, right? Defensive tackle for St. Louis Steamers?"

I nod, almost confused. "Yeah. How can I help you?"

She's holding a plate of food. "Sorry, I'm Jennifer—call me Jenna. Do you mind if I sit?"

I look down to where Aaron's plate is sitting. I nod and move it to the other side of me.

"Sorry, it's just—I had heard there were NFO players here, but I didn't believe it. But when one of my good friends started talking to Kyle Weaver, I changed my mind. He told us that you were here too." He props her head on the table with her arm and stares at me like I'm the bee's knees. "I didn't know it was common for NFO players to be so giving with their money."

My chest gets all tight. This woman is taking an interest in me because of my charity efforts. This was the whole reason I came here—to get attention like this and find a woman who I can actually keep by my side long-term. I know I just had a great evening with Aaron, but I'd be crazy to throw this opportunity away. Especially now that I've ruled out my sexuality as a reason for my inability to land a woman.

"Yeah," I say. "I'm actually still looking for different causes to donate to. Not to brag, but I have too much money to know what to do with. I figured someone else better have it."

She laughs and touches me playfully, shocking my whole body. It doesn't feel like how it does with Aaron—like a shot of electricity calibrated for me and only me—but it feels good nonetheless. Like I'm normal, accepted. Like I fit in. Exactly the opposite of how I felt when that woman years ago sneered at me for not keeping it hard.

"Well, me and my friend are here to present our specific research on a new way to conduct mammograms that we think is a better way to find breast cancer in women. We're presenting for the first session this morning if you want to come."

I shift in my seat. I promised Aaron that I would talk to him during the first session about funding his project. But here Jenna is presenting me with what I've wanted for years on a silver platter. Now that I've confirmed there's something deep inside me that repels women away, Jenna's behavior toward me proves that maybe hope isn't lost. Maybe, just as I planned, coming to this conference to bolster my image was the cure. Maybe now I can finally get a woman to like me and stick around.

And maybe Jenna is the woman who'll do that.

But just as I open my mouth to respond, Aaron comes waltzing into the room. He smiles at me and walks over to the table. My forehead starts to sweat as he sits down on my other side.

"Aaron, this is my friend Jenna," I say. "Jenna, this is Aaron."

"Nice to meet you Aaron," she says. "I research breast cancer over at Brigham and Women's in Boston." She looks at me with a smile that's definitely more than friendly. "I was just inviting Dominic here to attend our session this morning."

I glance at Aaron, and I can see his shoulders sinking like a falling tide.

"Session starts soon," she says, patting me on the hand. "I'm gonna go get ready. Can't wait to see you there."

Aaron pulls the plate in front of him, but he doesn't touch the food at all. He doesn't even bother opening up his syrup packets.

"I thought we were going to discuss my project," he says. "Was there a change of plans?"

I look down at my plate as I grind my jaw. I know I told Aaron that we were getting back together. But that was when I thought that being gay was the explanation for women not wanting me. Yet now that a woman clearly wants me, I can finally have a beautiful woman at my side. I'll be normal and no longer deserve ridicule.

I push my plate away and stand up. "I think I'm gonna check it out," I say, tossing my napkin on the table. "I wanna look around and see what the other projects are. We can talk later at lunch."

I have to look away from Aaron because his face is one of pure hurt.

He should understand this. I'm in the stinking NFO. I can't just announce I have a boyfriend. I'm not going to abandon him like he did me, but it's obviously much better for me to have a girlfriend. Maybe then he and I can have a friendship or something. But definitely not a partnership.

"Okay, fine," he says, his voice hardening. "Go."

My chest tightens hearing him so upset, and it keeps me standing there for another moment. I could run away and go see Jenna now. I could flirt with her, fund her project, then have the straight relationship I've always wanted, either with her or some other girl who's impressed with my charity efforts.

Or I could remember what pleasure I had with Aaron in bed. I could remember what an amazing relationship we had, and we could pick up where we left off.

But that's when I spot Kyle walking out of the big conference room. He's probably headed to Jenna's presentation. If Kyle Weaver, today's Sexiest Man Alive, has to find a woman, what hope is there for the rest of us who like men in the NFO?

And so I set off for Jenna's presentation.

Chapter 11

Aaron Watkins

Ice cold.

That's how Dominic looked at me when he decided to go to that redhead's project instead of discussing the funding of mine. It was like all the warmth and intimacy we had rekindled last night vanished into thin air.

Did I completely imagine last night? Was it really Dominic Johnson who I had sex with? Who held me in his arms all night? Who just decided to abandon me for some woman? Because I either slept with a complete stranger, or I don't know the man at all.

I pick at my eggs and sausage while sitting at the table alone, not even bothering to douse my plate in syrup. My appetite's completely dashed.

Or maybe there's a misunderstanding. Maybe he does really want to cover his bases by checking out other presentations. He said he would talk to me at lunch. My therapist always talks about not jumping to conclusions. Maybe I'll give it until then.

The last stragglers in the conference room are wrapping up their breakfast. I try to scarf down a few bites of my food so I don't skip meals like Dominic always says I do. Which, if he's really just abandoned me, fuck him. Fuck him for giving me the best sex of my life and then discarding me like I'm nothing, all while having reassured me by invoking the intimacy of our past relationship. He has no right to say try and be tender and take care of me if he just planned to use me as a quick fuck.

Calm down, Aaron. I take a deep breath, stand up, and take my food to the trash.

I don't know what Dominic's intentions are, so it's best to wait until lunchtime when he said he'll talk to me. I check the conference schedule and decide to go to the nearest presentation that sounds the most interesting. I just need to kill some time.

The first session I attend is on liver cancer. I try to focus on what the speakers are saying, but I keep going back to the sex from the night before. The way he took charge—I don't think I've ever had anyone fuck me like that. That was transcendent and so much more intimate than what he and I ever did. I think it just goes to show how much Dominic has changed over the years. But clearly that change isn't enough for him to really want me.

The next session isn't much better. I walk into a room about stomach cancer, which I know very little about. It just solidifies my uncertainty about whether or not I'll actually be able to find funding here. Everyone else is so competent. Maybe I'm just in over my head.

Finally, it's lunch time, and I speed to the conference hall. The line for the buffet is growing, so I get in line before it gets too long. I didn't eat much breakfast after all, and I'm starving. I search the room for Dominic and that redhead, but I don't see him anywhere. A pit forms in my stomach, and I start to sweat in uncomfortable places. *He could just be late,* I say to myself. *Don't jump to conclusions.*

Eventually, I get my food, and I sit down at a table out in the open so that Dominic will see me when he comes in. But I still don't see him. I could text him, but our relationship is still so fresh. Besides, I've only called him once since we've broken up. It just feels weird.

I sigh once I look around the room again and see no sign of him. If I don't see him by the end of lunch, I'll call him. And this isn't just about him funding my project. It's about us. Because the way he and that woman were eyeing each other makes me think that Dominic just decided he was straight. Talk about flipping the light switch.

And then I see him.

He and that redhead stroll through the hall entrance like they own the fucking place. The buffet line is gone, so they are free to casually grab their food.

My heart starts to race as they look for a table. I raise my hand, and that's when I catch his eye.

But he doesn't come my way.

He points to another table, says something to the redhead, and then she leaves him to sit down.

My heart feels like it's going to burst through my chest.

The bastard saw me. He knows I'm over here. And now he's gonna pretend like he never did.

But then he walks toward me, and I don't know if I should be relieved or even more angry. Because something tells me he's not coming here to stay.

"Hey," he says, sheepishly looking around, still standing.

"What's the deal?" I say, standing up in a rushed whisper. "You say you're going to meet with me and then you ditch me for some girl?"

He rubs the bridge of his nose, still holding his plate. He hasn't set it down, so I know for sure he's not sitting with me. He's gonna go sit with her.

"It's complicated," he says.

"Really?" I hiss. "That's all you're going to say?" I look around, then step closer, worried someone will hear us. "Dominic, last night was amazing. But this morning you were as cold as a blizzard. You said we wanted to try us for real. But now it feels like you're dating this girl. What are you about?"

He sucks on his lips, and he puts on a face so distressed I can practically hear the gears in his mind working on overdrive.

"I feel used," I continue. "Like you just wanted a lay. And now that you got what you want, you're just throwing me away."

He looks me dead in the eyes. "That's not it at all."

"Then what is it?" I ask.

He turns, and the redhead is waving for him to come join her. Then he turns back to me.

"Look," he says definitively. "This is complicated. And this isn't easy for me. But I don't think, uh, this can work. At least the way you were hoping."

"I was hoping?" I ask, scoffing. "You were the one who wanted to try this again."

"I know," he says, digging his palm into his forehead. "It's just—I want you in my life. I care about you a lot. And part of me believes I love you. But I just don't think I want this."

I let out a sharp laugh. "Well at least you're honest. Wow."

He puts his hand on my arm. "Look, I still want to be friends. Like I said, you're important to me and—"

I pull away from him like his hand is barbed. "You don't get to decide that," I say, disgusted. And not knowing what else to do, I storm away.

"Aaron," he says. "Aaron," he calls out louder. But I don't turn back. I just barrel into the hallway. I want to go to the elevators and go back to my room and just cry into my pillows. But that's Dominic's room too. So I pull out my phone and call the only one I can.

"Hey Aaron," Laura says when I answer.

"Can we go get lunch?" I ask. "I need to talk to you."

"Absolutely," she says. "I was about to go." She's been eating out because her pregnancy has made her pretty picky. "I'll drop a pin."

"See you soon."

* * *

"Jesus H. Christ," Laura says after having just taken a huge bite out of her chicken tender. "I'm aghast that you didn't tell me this sooner. So you dated an NFO player in college?"

"Well, he wasn't in the NFO *at the time.*"

"Same thing," she says, still chewing. "And fate makes you both share a room? That is fucking ridiculous."

I roll my eyes. "Tell me about it."

"And now he's going hot and cold."

"I think he's landed and is staying on cold," I say.

Laura takes another bite of her chicken tender and squints at something random, thinking.

We're sitting at table in one of those colorful restaurants where the staff randomly break into Broadway songs. This would be Laura's first pick.

"I'm concluding he's an asshole," she says.

I sigh, and I feel like a balloon having lost all this air.

Then a waitress jumps up onto the back of a booth. The lights go dark and a spotlight shines on her, and then she starts singing "Satisfied" from *Hamilton*.

"Holy shit, she's good," Laura says, eating her fries like popcorn.

As we watch the waitress, I mull over my feelings.

Part of me came here to have Laura encourage me. To help me see that maybe there was hope in this situation. She's the romantic, after all: marrying in grad school, crying at the end of every musical. I thought she would see some hope in Dominic. But apparently not.

Laura shoots up, hitting the table with her bump. I have to hold in place as she furiously claps for the waitress.

"Bravo!" she yells, then she sits down. "You look sad," she says when notices me. And she's right. I've hardly even touched my milkshake, let alone my burger and fries.

"I'm just disappointed," I say.

"Of course you would be," she says. "Your old flame betrayed you. He wasn't who you thought he was."

"But what if there's still some good in him?" I ask. "Part of me wants to run away. But another part wants to give him another chance."

She chews on her lips as she nods. "You know, years ago I would have told you to never trust people like Dominic." She sighs, almost laughing. "And then I met Patrick."

"Here we go," I say jokingly. I love it when she talks about how she fell in love with her husband.

"Patrick and I met in high school, and we had dated on and off for years. There were times I thought he was ready for a relationship, but then he'd show in some ways that he wasn't. Or I would do the same. It wasn't until my third year of grad school that we had grown tired of chasing each other. We decided to be adults and give it one last shot, having completely gotten all of the jitters about the relationship out of our system."

"And that's when it worked," I say.

"And now I'm pregnant!" she says.

"But could that happen with Dominic?"

She squints at me. "Definitely not the pregnant part."

I roll my eyes and can't help but laugh. "The relationship part, I mean."

She frowns and looks down the table, thinking. "I don't know. But honestly, Aaron, it doesn't sound like it. He just left you for some girl. He said himself it couldn't work."

I deflate into my seat, and there's a painful tightening in my chest. It feels like I'm experiencing Dominic pushing me away all over again.

"So I was really right to break up with him years ago," I say. "He was just going to abandon me like I thought."

"But I could be wrong," she says. "There were some moments I thought it could never work out with Patrick again."

"So what are you saying?"

"I'm saying that if you really want him again, be open to opening things with him again. But don't force it. Like you said, you don't want to be used. So don't be used. Focus on you. You're here to find funding, after all. Not a boyfriend. Focus on that. And let the rest of it settle into place."

I chew on her words, nodding. They feel right.

"Just try not to be like Angelica Schuyler," she says.

I look up with a furrowed brow, a smile forming on my face. This wouldn't be a conversation with Laura if a musical wasn't referenced.

"You know," Laura says, gesturing to the waitress who just performed the number. "She'll never be satisfied? You don't have to be like her. You can be open to a future possibility with Dominic again. Take advantage of an opportunity to talk to him again if it arises. You don't have to write him off completely. Just don't forgo your own wants and desires for him."

"Huh," I say. "I don't know how you always make musicals relate, but you just do."

She bows. "They should have me singing here."

I laugh. And then I feel my phone buzzing. I pull it out, thinking it's Dominic. But it's the last person I was expecting.

"Is that him?" Laura asks.

"No," I say. I scan the text twice to be sure. "It's the investor I was supposed to meet with last night. And he's open to get dinner."

"There you go," Laura says. "See? Things work out."

I nod as I text him back. "They sure do," I say. And when I hit send, a burst of hope shoots through me. I may not get a boyfriend out of this trip, but at the very least, I have a chance at funding. And while I don't want to try and win my parents love so much anymore, I do want to honor my sister's legacy with my research. And now that this investor wants to meet with me again, I now have another chance of doing it.

Chapter 12

Dominic Johnson

I KNOW THAT FINALLY having a girl want to date me should feel amazing. I should be euphoric. That's why I came to this conference after all, right? And I didn't even think I would find one this early. I've got the respect of a woman now. I should feel happy. I got what I wanted.

So why do I feel like absolute dogshit?

I sit with Jenna as we watch one of her colleagues' presentations. Kyle Weaver's also here with that woman he was flirting with earlier. I try to pay attention, but there's a dark cloud of sadness weighing down my brain, making it hard to focus.

I hardly ever curse. It just feels useless and vulgar. But now there couldn't be a better time. Because I don't know what the hell is wrong with me.

"Come on," Jenna says when the presentation is over. I'm so out of it that I couldn't even tell it was done.

"Let's go congratulate her," she says. "Support her as potential donors ask her questions."

"Fine," I say standing up and following her.

Even now that I have everything I want, it feels like something is missing. This entire time, I've thought I needed a woman. Memories of my night with Aaron flash through my mind, and they act like umbrellas to the dark storm that is my mood, protecting me on occasion from the rains of sadness. When I think of

Aaron, I feel good. Happy. But when I think about a life with Jenna, my mind gets dark and stormy.

I know I just met her, but let's be honest, that's where it would lead: marriage, children, and so on. If not with her then with another woman. I know this is something that I've been wanting for the past several years, but now that I have it, I'm not so sure I want it anymore.

In between chats with investors, Jenna gets the chance to talk to her friend. I pretend I have to take an important call and step to the side. And that's when I can hear them talking about me. Her friend's asking if I'm really with the NFO, and Jenna's saying I am. That I'm interested in helping pay for one of her projects.

And suddenly I get a sick feeling inside.

Aaron said I used him. But I definitely didn't. I just realized he wasn't what I wanted.

But Jenna—is she using me? For my money and my image?

"Hey," Jenna says, coming up to me. I fake hangup on whoever I was pretend talking to.

"Vanessa wants to go to dinner with some of our friends. You want to join? You could meet some of my colleagues, some others that will work on the project."

I mull it over. I don't see why not. Meeting her friends and colleagues makes sense if I'm gonna fund her project, even more if we're to date. So why is it that I want to go into my room and curl into a ball? And hope that Aaron walks in so I can apologize and make love with him again? No, I can't to do that. I let him go. I'm on my own now.

"Sure," I say. "Sounds fun."

And boy is it not.

We eat at some fancy restaurant, and it's me, Jenna, and a handful of her colleagues from Harvard. As all of them laugh and talk with one another, it feels like I'm watching myself from afar. Like I've died and now I'm watching my lifeless body go through the motions. More than anything, I want to run away. I want to call Aaron up and talk with him. After hard practices or games, he was always the first person I wanted to talk to. And that definitely hasn't changed over the years. But now that I've had a taste of him again and had to let him go, this desire for him has grown from a campfire to a bonfire in my chest.

"You doing okay?" Jenna asks me while her friends talk with one another.

I try my best to shake from my stupor, but it's getting more difficult by the minute to fake any enthusiasm. How am I supposed to do this for my whole life? Why did I ever think this was what I wanted?

"Yeah," I say. "Just tired I think. Haven't been sleeping well." Which is the biggest lie of this weekend. Sleeping with Aaron in my arms has been like taking a shot of sleep-inducing cold medicine.

Shoot. Aaron's still my roommate. My *bedmate*, for Pete's sake. Which means I'm definitely going to see him again on this trip. I swear I'll crumble to pieces if I have to see his sweet, hurt face just one more time.

Jenna puts her hand on my thigh, and it takes all my strength not to jump away from her. "We can get out of here if you want," she says. Her finger trails up to my crotch.

For the love of all that's holy. I know I should be over the moon right now. A woman wants to sleep with me. I could pack up my things and head home to St. Louis with this confidence. I've earned a woman's affection.

But her touch just makes me sick to my stomach.

She leans over to whisper in my ear. "There's no one else rooming with me," she says. "So we could have some nice, private time."

Her hand hovers just over my crotch, and I swear that my penis could not be softer than in this moment.

But she is offering me a place to stay. Which means I won't have to sleep with Aaron.

"Let's do it," I say. I look around, and her friends are still deep in conversation. Judging by how long we've been here, I bet we'd have a least another hour if we organically let this night end. "Let's go now."

Jenna eagerly smiles, then turns to her friends to say goodbye. The waiter comes with a check, and I take out my wallet to pay. But when I see the receipt, I freeze.

In my dissociation, I didn't pay attention to what these women were order-ing. But scanning the receipt shows me they ordered the most expensive things on the menu. Things that I know even a researcher from Harvard shouldn't be able to afford. I told Jenna and her friends that dinner would be my treat, but that doesn't mean they can rack up my bill.

The feeling that I'm being used creeps up my spine again. I'm not sure if I can live a life in a relationship where I feel so sad and empty. But a relationship where I'm used for my money? That just makes me pure angry. It also makes me wonder why I'm doing this whole 'finding a woman' thing in the first place. Was this what I was chasing this whole time? An empty relationship devoid of affection and care? I don't understand how the NFO can't accept gay relationships, yet they can accept sad relationships like these.

"Ready?" Jenna asks once the waiter returns with my card.

I sigh, annoyed that neither her nor her friends have offered to help pay. "Let's get out of here."

On our way back to the hotel, Jenna reaches out to hold my hand. Now that I'm with a woman, I willingly hold her hand in return, but it feels like a bitter cloud of ash rises in my chest when I do.

I wish it was Aaron's hand that I was holding. Not Jenna's. And I wish I held his hand on our way back from that date last night. And there's a small, small part of me that wishes I never walked away from him in the first place.

Once we're back in the hotel, dread pools in my stomach as I know, only minutes from now, I'm gonna have to have sex with Jenna.

And that's when my heart starts to race.

How the hell am I going to get hard with her? When Jenna gets anywhere close to me, my penis practically shrivels up. Which doesn't make sense, because she is beautiful. But seeing the way Jenna is and the way she talks to her friends, I worry she'll be just like the girl who laughed at me for not being able to stay hard.

My forehead breaking into a sweat, I look around the foyer of the hotel as we walk to the elevator, anything to get me out of this. At the hotel bar, I spot Kyle Weaver, but there's an unexplainable sadness about him. He's frowning down at his half-empty glass of what looks like whiskey, thumbing the circle. I would go over and chat with him, stalling my time with Jenna. But something tells me he just wants to be alone right now.

Guess it's time for sex after all.

Once we reach Jenna's floor, she holds my hand as we head to her room. Inside, I take in her strong scent: mangoes and lilac. In front of the bed, she hooks her arms around my neck and looks up at me.

"Uh, I stink," I say, willing to say anything to get her off me.

She uncurls herself and half-scowls.

"Sorry," I say. "Mind if I shower first?"

"Sure," she says, sitting down on the bed. "That'll give me time to call my sister."

"Great," I say, genuinely relieved that I'm successfully procrastinating this. I make my way past the sink and towel rack and into the bathroom. I close the door with a heavy sigh, then turn on the shower. I sit down on the toilet as I let the hot water steam up the room, still in the clothes I wore to dinner.

I don't know if I could be sadder. But I did ask for this. I turned down the man that I loved—who I realized I still love—all for some life I was too afraid of not having. But now that I have it, I don't want it. But I don't know what to do about it.

Not wanting the water to get cold, I stand up to go grab a towel from outside the bathroom before I step in the shower.

But then I hear Jenna say my name.

I pause and listen, trying to tune out the sound of the water to hear her more clearly.

"...he's really cute, yeah," she says. "Mhm."

I shrug. At least she thinks I'm handsome.

"Yes, he's loaded," she says, as if this was some expectation her sister had of her in finding a man. "You should have seen the platinum card he used to pay for dinner. Once I get him to officially fund my project, I'll have him locked in for good."

My chest tightens, and my stomach sinks to the floor.

So she is using me.

Towel in hand, I go back into the bathroom, and I'm about to strip and get into the shower. But then I stop myself.

I could bury my head in the sand and pretend I heard nothing. I could shower, have sex with Jenna, and get the straight life I've always wanted, one free from shame and ridicule.

Or I could do what I really want and run away now, putting my life on a whole new trajectory. I don't know what that would look like, but in thinking about now, any life is far preferable to this dreadful one I'm about to embark on. Women are fine, but I just can't live my life with one. I can't.

I walk back out of the bathroom, and Jenna is talking with her sister about the vacations she'll be able to go on. I know I should be upset that she's indeed using me for my money, but I'm not. Because I'm honestly not surprised. There were signs of this earlier. And to be quite frank, I'm relieved. Because now I'm justified in doing what I'm about to do.

I step out of the bathroom and set the towel gently back on the rack, then shut the door to the bathroom as quietly as I can. Then, out of her line of sight, I open Jenna's room door and slip out into the hallway, all while she's yapping to her sister about the lifestyle I'll be able to afford her. Sorry, Jenna. I don't think you'll get your dream life after all. At least with me.

After I shut the door, I fast-walk until I reach the elevators, and I don't feel safe until I'm completely inside. Once the doors shut, I just sit there, my back against the wall, taking deep breaths. Luckily, I never actually gave Jenna any of my contact info. So I think that was the last of her. Somehow, I've made it out of the straight life that I have been chasing for years. And I couldn't feel more relieved.

When I've composed myself, I look down at the buttons. I could go back to the sixth floor, but that's where Aaron will be. I don't know if I'm ready to see him now or ever. But where else could I go?

Seeing I have no other option, I press the ground floor button and hope that my old friend is still there. When I reach the lobby, I stroll over to the bar, and there he is, still with the same glass but now empty. And he has a forlorn expression on his face.

"Dominic Johnson," he says, looking up at me. He seems genuinely happy to see me, but only so much so, as if there's a low limit to his joy right now.

"Kyle Weaver," I say, taking the stool next to him. "What's going on? Looks like you've seen hell."

He chuckles. "You swear now, huh?" His accent is always so much stronger when he's drunk, as rarely as he is.

"After what I've been through on this trip, I might as well," I say. The bartender asks what I want, and I just order us some waters. Kyle and I were never too much into drinking back at Miss U. Which is why I'm surprised he's so wasted now.

"Thanks," Kyle says to the bartender when he drops off the water. He takes a big gulp, then sighs. "Women, man." He shakes his head, then looks up to the bottles on the wall as if they have the answer to all his troubles. The bartender takes his glass and fills it up with some more whiskey.

"Women, what?" I ask after the bartender's gone.

"Dominic," he says like a teacher about to start their lesson. "Don't be like me."

My stomach jumps. "What do you mean?"

"I mean that you shouldn't try to have what I have," he says. "No one should."

My blood runs cold. Does he know that I'm trying to follow in his footsteps to get a good image? To get women to like me?

He picks up his whiskey and swirls it in the glass. "You ever get that dark feeling around women?"

I perk up. "Yes," I say, not even caring to temper my answer. Because I'm so relieved I'm not the only one.

"I think some guys like you and me—guys who were part of our little club at Miss U—are not meant to find a woman. I think we're going against who we really are. Course, there are some guys who like both men and women. But most of us just deny that part of ourselves—the part that like men." He lets out a bitter laugh. "To what end, though? To fit in?"

To not be made fun of, I think. *To not feel the shame of being less than a man.*

"I don't know," I say.

He takes a sip of his whiskey, then sets down his glass. He sets down some cash that seems to be much more than his bill and stands up.

"I'm tired of this dark feeling," he says. Then he looks right at me, his posture teetering. "If you get the chance, don't be like me. Find someone who doesn't make you feel like your world is going to end. Even if they're a man."

He hiccups, then holds himself against the counter. I stand up and put my arm around his shoulder.

"Alright, buddy, let's get you back to your room."

He puts his arm around me, and then we wish the bartender a goodnight as we head to the elevators. Even though he looks like he's about to pass out, he manages to hand me his card and tell me his room number. Luckily, the lobby is mostly empty, everyone either out at dinner or in their rooms, so no one will see us like this.

When we reach Kyle's room, I help him lay down on the bed closest to the door. And that's when I see there are two beds in here. Gosh darn it, man. How'd they manage to stuff me and Aaron into the same room with one bed and then let Kyle have two beds to himself? I'll never understand how the universe makes things happen.

I see a bottle of over-the-counter painkillers on the dresser, so I pick them up and set them on Kyle's nightstand.

"Drink up and take some of these," I say, sitting down on the other bed. "It'll help you in the morning."

Kyle sits up and opens the bottle of pills. "Just like Miss U," he says. He takes four pills and chugs the water like a pro.

"Except you hardly ever got this drunk," I say. "Kinda worried about you, man."

Still fully clothed, he lifts up the covers and buries himself underneath them. "As I said," he says, nuzzling himself in the pillow. "If I could just find someone who didn't make my mind all dark, I'd be golden. It's just a shame I can't find a woman who makes me feel that way."

I chew on my lips, wishing to respond, but I have nothing to say.

"You want the other bed?" Kyle says, already sounding half asleep.

I look at it, then nod. "Yeah, please," I say. "I don't have anywhere else to stay tonight."

"Have at it," he says. And then he shuts his eyes, and I know I'm by myself now.

I strip down to my underwear and slip under the covers. I turn off the lights and rest my head on the pillow, but I couldn't sleep if I wanted. My body is exhausted, but my brain is wide awake.

Kyle Weaver, the Sexiest Man Alive—the man who could find a woman more easily than anyone—doesn't want one. He's recommending I don't pursue a woman if it doesn't feel right. And after my experience with Jessica, I know that no woman is right for me.

So does that mean Aaron is?

None of this makes sense. I start out thinking I bolster my image so I can finally get a woman who'll stick with me for the long haul. Then, after realizing my feelings for Aaron, I think that women don't like me because they can sense I'm gay. Then I rule that out because Kyle Weaver is the same as me but can get any girl he wants. So I think I'm cursed. But then once I finally get what I've wanted all these years—a woman interested in me—I realize that the straight life isn't for me.

Kyle mentioned the darkness that comes over his mind whenever he tries to connect with a woman. And that's exactly how I feel, too, which is crazy. I thought I was the only one. And thinking about what this means, I'm starting to realize there has never been a curse at all.

Whenever I was in a relationship with a woman, I, too, would get that dark cloud in my head. Then, as I always saw it happening, the woman would leave me. And I thought it was because of *her* issues. But now I realize it was always the other way around. I was the one who, depressed by the dark cloud in my mind, would pull away from my girlfriends, icing them out until they had no choice but to leave me. In other words, I was the reason relationships were ending, but it wasn't because I was cursed. It was because I was gay. It was because, deep down, I knew I didn't want them.

The realization hits me like a damn breaking, making me tired enough to sleep. And as I close my eyes, I realize there's only one person I do want.

I let my mind drift to my time with Aaron the night before. How his coldness toward me gradually turned to warmth, how I finally got him to open up and smile at dinner, how we got to reminisce over old times together. Gosh, he made me so happy.

When I was with Jenna, the thought of Aaron was like an umbrella protecting me against the rain of sadness. And that was just thinking about him. Imagine what giving the relationship a try would look like—a genuine try this time. He wouldn't just be an umbrella. Since I'd be pursuing somebody I wanted, the clouds would be gone, and he would be like the water cooling my skin while swimming on a hot day. In other words, he'd make life better for me. Not worse.

Slowly, sleep gradually overcomes me, and I'm reminded again of what Kyle's just told me: I should find someone who doesn't bring on the storms in my head. Luckily, I now know who that is. So, if Kyle, the Sexiest Man Alive who can get anyone he wants, is recommending this to me, it's all but certain what I should do next. And now that I know I'm gay through and through, I can finally do it with all my heart.

I sigh contentedly, ready to sleep and for the morning to come. Because that's when I'm gonna go get Aaron Watkins back.

Chapter 13

Aaron Watkins

ON MY WAY TO the restaurant where I'm meeting the investor, Bill, for dinner, I check the address he sent against the address I'm headed to for the fourth time. There is no way in hell I'm making the mistake of going to the wrong place again.

When I reach the restaurant, I see the investor sitting at a nearby table, and I breathe a sigh of relief. I haven't screwed up my chances at funding.

Yet.

"There you are," he says, standing to shake my hand.

"Sorry I'm late," I say, pulling of my bag and setting it against my chair.

He glances at his watch. "You're not," he says. "It's five 'til seven."

"Just didn't want to keep you waiting," I say as we both sit down. "Sorry if you've been here for long. I'm really grateful you're taking the time to meet with me again after what happened yesterday."

"Oh, don't worry about that," he says with a swat of his hand. "We're both adults here. Life happens. I'm glad we could work it out too. Your research really intrigues me."

I perk up at that. "It still does?"

"Oh yeah," he says with the nod of his head. "I've been to a lot of presentations and heard a lot of people talk about what they do. And you're the one who interests me the most."

My stomach jumps as if I'm in free fall, and I think I'm blushing. "Well, thank you."

The waitress comes to take our order, and then Bill leans forward and rests his elbows on the table. It's time to talk business.

"How's the conference been for you?" he asks. "I'm sure you're swimming in offers."

I try to resist frowning. I don't know if being honest about my success makes me or my research look bad, but it also feels shameful just to lie about it. So I just decide to tell the truth.

"Well, my presentation isn't until tomorrow, so no one's heard everything I have to say. But I also haven't had much luck. You're really the only person who's expressed interest enough to speak with me."

I expect him to frown at that, to rethink all the effort he's put forth to meet with me. But I swear there's a sparkle in his eye, and he leans forward even further.

"Then I'm so glad I caught you before the presentation," he says. "Because I'm the first to take up on what I think will be field-changing research."

My eyes widen. "What are you talking about?"

He takes a sip of his cocktail, then looks at me with a furrowed brow. "You're telling me you don't see the potential?"

Shame flushes through me. "I—I don't know. I know that my treatment could be potentially lead to a more productive use of chemotherapy for children with leukemia—"

"Productive?" Bill says, almost scoffing. But there's a smile there. "I always forget how modest you academic researchers are. Never seeing your work for what it truly is."

My stomach tumbles over itself, and I don't know if I should be excited or ashamed. "I'm sorry, I don't think I understand."

"Sure, sure," he says, almost condescendingly. "Aaron, I know leukemia like the back of my hand. I have an MD myself. I've also met with many people in your field, specifically studying leukemia. I've talked with academics at Harvard, Johns Hopkins, Columbia. All obviously smart, but they're all stuck in their ways. You, however—you've got a fresh angle with your research. And I know enough about your field to be confident in saying that your research won't just lead to a more productive use of chemotherapy. No. It could lead to a use of chemotherapy that could cure leukemia entirely."

My blood goes cold, and I can hear my heart race in my ears. "I'm sorry—you're saying that my research into the enhancing our current forms of chemotherapy can lead to curing leukemia?" I'm so surprised that my words don't even sound like my own.

"Exactly," he says.

Our food arrives, but I hardly notice. My mind is racing so fast that the Avengers themselves could be destroying the street outside and I wouldn't even care to look.

I could arrive at the *cure* to leukemia with my research. Not a treatment that could make remission easier or life prolonged. But the cure. I must have been so buried in my research that I didn't see the potential. And didn't Dominic say this was what I was capable of just before we kissed? I just blew him off then, thinking he was just trying to flatter me. But he may have been right.

"I—I don't know what to say. This is what I've been chasing my whole career. I just didn't think I'd find it this early, if at all."

"You should be proud of yourself," he says. "And I don't say that lightly. I don't know how other academics don't see the promise in your research. It's so alarmingly clear to me and my colleagues that I've spoken with that I can say it confidently to you."

"Wow," I say, shaking my head. I have enough of my senses to come back to reality and get more information. "So, if we were to work together to see this cure through, what would be the budget for the project? The timeline."

"I'd say we'd expect the prototypical treatment to be ready in the next three years."

I feel like I've been punched in the gut. Three years would be a steep turnaround for an expert with decades of experience in the field and dozens of researchers at their side. All I have is me and maybe some graduate research assistants.

"But—"

He puts up his hand to stop me. "And you'd be receiving all the funding you'd need."

"I'm sorry," I say. "What?"

He sighs, almost impatient. "Your funding would be nearly unlimited for you to achieve this quick goal. You could get as many research assistants, equipment, and subjects as you would need."

I let out a laugh. "I'm sorry," I say. "This is just—are you serious? This is too good to be true."

"I mean every word," he says matter-of-factly. And it looks like he's growing tired of explaining it.

"I—this is wonderful. Amazing. I'd obviously need to review the contract and go over it with my colleagues, but I don't see how I could say no."

"Great," he says with a nod. "This might be the most profitable decision you'll ever make in your lifetime."

I freeze. "Profitable?"

"What?" he asks, pulling his arms off the table. "You think you'll be able to come up with cure for leukemia and not patent it? By setting it at a competitive price, you could easily become a billionaire in your lifetime."

Excitement leaves my body as dread gradually pours into me like fresh cement, weighing me down in my chair. Of course such an offer is too good to be true.

After seeing how medical bills destroyed my family, I vowed to never put the same burden on anyone else. And I plan on sticking to that vow—even if that means not profiting from the cure to leukemia.

"I—you have to understand. I set out to research leukemia with the hope that I could provide treatment—or the cure—free-of-charge. Besides, what good is a cure to a family with a sick child if they're then steeped in medical debt?"

Bill grunts. "I thought since your research was so genius, you'd be a little savvier when it came to business," he says. "But I guess it's wise not to over-estimate academics. You have to understand that we live in a society where innovation moves us forward, but at a cost. And you are one of the lucky few who will prosper from this cost."

"Yeah, at the expense of thousands of children and families."

"Who will happily pay any price to save their loved ones. Think about this—you'd be a fool to turn this down. Besides, you said it yourself—I'm the only one who's given you a funding offer. No one else sees the potential in your research like I do. You'd regret walking away from this conference having turned down your only offer, the offer that could have made you a hero and set you up for life. With me, you'd be a legend in your discipline, and you'd never have to worry about money again."

I fold my arms and sit there as the restaurant bustles around me.

I could take his offer. I could develop the first cure for leukemia and save the lives of thousands of children, maybe hundreds of thousands over my lifetime. But at what cost? I know what this man means when he says 'competitive price'. Poor, traumatized families finally free of the shackles of leukemia would then be saddled with hundreds of thousands of dollars, leaving them with just as much stress as leukemia itself. Sure, their child would be alive, and there might be some who could afford it or crowd source funds, but they'd be in the minority. The medical debt would crush nearly everyone who chose the cure.

If my family had the cure, we'd have been over the moon. But we had a ton of money trouble as it was when Lorie was going through chemo. This money trouble was the final kicker that turned my parents into the zombies they became after Lorie died. If I were to put this financial burden on families with children receiving this treatment, I'd be effectively consigning them to the same fate as my family. And that's the exact opposite thing I set out to do.

"I'm sorry," I say, pushing out my chair. "I can't do this."

"Are you serious?" he says. "You're really going to throw this opportunity away? I'm the only chance you have."

"I'm not patenting the cure to leukemia," I say. "And I won't agree to an investor until they accept those terms."

Bill shoots up and throws his napkin on the table. "Well I hope you can live with depriving the world of the cure," he says. "Because nobody's gonna fund you without a patent."

I scowl, surprised by this supposed professional's harsh words. "I'm sorry, but—"

He shakes his hand at me and grabs his things. "I wish you the best," he says. "But clearly we have nothing more to talk about here." And then he storms out of the restaurant, leaving me to foot the bill.

I sit there for a minute, shocked that all this just happened. I even think about chasing after him and asking for a compromise, but my gut tells me not to. He seemed sure of himself. And I'm definitely not backing down from my 'no patent' stance. I feel a bit shaky, but I know I did the right thing. I know it. So I decide to stay here and finish my meal. I'm hungry after skipping breakfast and not eating most of my lunch, after all.

As I finish up my pasta, I reflect on my options.

I just rejected the only sure lead I had to get funding for my research. But there are positives. First, I know that my research is incredibly promising—not just promising, actually, but miraculous. I may have discovered the cure for leukemia. If anything, I should be grateful that I had this conversation with Bill. He helped me see that.

Second, I still have the opportunity to present my research with this new insight, which gives me another chance of finding an investor. While he was my only chance at funding so far, he was only trying to scare me by saying that. I still have the chance to find someone else with my presentation.

The waitress comes with the check, and I grimace at the price. Maybe it's best I didn't work with this guy. That's what Dominic said, right? How he was a poor communicator? Making me foot the entire bill isn't a great sign either. I think Dominic was right. I dodged a bullet.

Dominic.

While I wait for the waitress to return my card, I can't get him off my mind. Back in college, he was the one I'd go to after a long, stressful day. He always knew what to say to calm me down, to make me feel at home. Even though he totally tossed me aside for a girl, I still miss him. In fact, I've been missing him all these years. I just didn't want to accept it.

Once I get my card back, I wipe my mouth and begin the trek back to my hotel. Dominic's probably rooming with that redhead, which is good. I'm not ready to see him at all. So I plan on just getting in bed and passing out.

Part of me wants to reach out to him now, but that doesn't feel right. He's the one who walked away from me. I should give us both the dignity to let him come to terms with his actions and apologize himself. Like Laura said, if it feels right, I can reach out first. But I have my own business to take care of. Tomorrow, I have to convince a bunch of investors, tired after a long conference, that I may just have the cure for leukemia. And that they should fund me without looking for profit.

My stomach churns as I walk, and I can feel a headache coming on from the pressure. Then I take a deep breath, steeling myself. I'm doing this for Lorie, for myself, and for all families that suffer from a loved one with cancer. This is motivation sufficient to get me through. Something will work out. I can feel it.

Chapter 14

Dominic Johnson

I WAKE UP ALONE in Kyle Weaver's extra bed with a clear head and specific goal. I messed up with Aaron Watkins. I pushed him away, thinking my life was supposed to be with a woman. But now that I have that knocked out as a possibility, I know it's him that I want. I just need to apologize first.

I get up from bed and start putting on the clothes I wore the day before. They stink, but I guess this is what I get for walking out on the man that I love to chase some random woman. Kyle's in the other bed still sound asleep. During the night, it looks like he's managed to strip off his clothes because they're scattered around his bed. I'd wake him to say goodbye, but with how much he drank last night, I'll give him all the space he needs. I hope that he finds someone who doesn't cast such a shadow in his mind someday. And I'm just grateful that I have mine. I hope he'll take me back.

Once I'm dressed, I make my way out of Kyle's and head for the elevator to the sixth floor. I'm hoping to find Aaron before he heads to breakfast. I know he has his big presentation today, and I want to give him as much time before then to process what I'm asking for.

By the time I reach his door, I'm nearly shaking in my shoes.

I did hurt Aaron. But he's not a mean guy. At the very least, he'll want to talk to me too, right? He won't push me away? Gosh, even though that's exactly what I did to him. God, please give me the strength to do this. And give Aaron the patience to deal with me.

I scan my key card and slowly open the door. The first thing I see is Aaron dressed up in a freshly ironed suit adjusting his tie in the mirror above the dresser. I swear he's gotten more handsome in the last twenty-four hours.

He turns to see me, then freezes. "Dominic," he says, then pulls his tie tight.

"I know you probably weren't expecting to see me," I say.

"Honestly, I didn't know what I was expecting from you," he says. "You've been pretty unpredictable."

I sigh. "Fair enough. Do you have time to talk?"

He glances at the bedside clock. "I got a little time before breakfast. You know my presentation's today, right? I wanna get enough to eat and give myself plenty of time to prepare. I still haven't found funding."

"Of course," I say, stepping further into the room. "And I wouldn't miss it for the world."

Aaron ignores my attempt to connect and sits down in the lone voyeur chair, leaving me to sit on the bed by myself. "What did you want to say?" he asks.

I adjust myself on the bed, just so happening to sit right on the part where I first put myself inside Aaron. Man, he felt good. I hope that wasn't the last time that'll happen. Not just 'cause I want to have sex with him. But because I really think I love him.

"I was wrong to push you away yesterday," I say. "I recognize I did exactly what your parents did to you and what you did to me. I walked away with little to no explanation."

Aaron sighs through my nose. "Just after you asked to get back together too," he says. "I was really confused."

"And you know what? I was too." I shake my head. "You gotta understand. I grew up religious in Georgia. Being gay wasn't really an option for me. There was so much shame around it. And I'll be honest: you were the exception to that, but after you left me, I didn't want to date anyone. I fooled around with some guys who prefer I keep their identity secret, but after that, I just decided that the whole gay thing was a phase. That I could move on and grow up from it. That way I wouldn't have to deal with the ridicule I always saw gay people deal with."

Aaron scoffs. "So what? I didn't mean anything to you?"

"You meant everything to me, Aaron. But I did what I could to explain away what we had after you left me. I called you my best friend. My buddy. My friend turned more than friend. I thought this would get you out of my head, but I was clearly wrong."

"But it seemed like you had no issue moving onto women. What was your deal with that redhead yesterday?"

I sigh and rub my forehead. "She was a mistake. See, I'll tell you why I really came here. I thought I could be just like star linebacker Kyle Weaver. I thought I could enhance my reputation by finding some cancer charity to donate to like he does so I could get a woman. Because it felt like no woman was really interested in me."

He raises an eyebrow. "*You* were having trouble with finding a woman?"

I can't help but blush at that. It makes me happy to know that Aaron Watkins thinks I'm a stud, even after everything.

"And with Jenna, I finally had it. But it turned out it wasn't what I wanted."

"And what do you want?" Aaron asks, crossing his arms.

I take a minute thinking it over just to be sure, and I don't open my mouth until I'm 100% confident. "You," I finally say.

Aaron thins his lips, and he looks away, probably thinking.

"See, I was talking with a friend about this," I say, keeping Kyle's identity a secret for now. "He's like me, you know—a gay man in the NFO. He described to me an experience he's had, and it's the exact same with me—how when I need to be intimate around a woman, I freeze up, and my brain gets all dark, like there's a storm inside my head."

Aaron nods, still looking away. But he's listening.

"He told me that if I ever could, I should run away from intimacy like this," I continue. "I should instead find people who don't make me feel like I have a storm in my head but like the opposite—like the sun is shining on a bright summer's day. And after thinking it over, I realized that I wanted this. And that you were my sun on a bright summer's day."

Aaron's chewing on his lips, still thinking.

"So I want to try it again. For real this time."

He looks at me, and I nearly shrivel under his gaze. But I manage to keep sitting tall. I want him to see that I really mean it.

"You know I think I believe you when you say this," he says.

And my chest soars.

"But the thing is," he continues. "I've heard this all before. This is so similar to what you told me when we went out to dinner."

"Because I meant it then too."

"But if you meant it, why did you run away to be with Jenna? You left me high-and-dry, Dominic."

"I ran away because I didn't know that's what I didn't need. But I couldn't know that until I tried. Now I know I'm gay and it's you who I want."

He shakes his head. "I don't know, Dominic. How can I know that you won't just walk out on me again? If you get scared? Or if someone finds out about us?"

I close my eyes and breathe out an almost painful sigh. "I don't know what I can give you beside my word. But I give that to you 100%. I won't run away from you again."

He lifts his fist to his mouth to bite on his knuckles, and he stares outside at the street below. Then he sighs, and I know he's about to give his final answer.

"I don't think I can trust you," he says. "With my parents—you know. I need someone who I can trust and won't just walk out on me. And you did that to me just as I let you back into my life. I don't know if I can deal with that again."

Sorrow shoots through my body in the form of tightening muscles, but I try my best to keep my cool. Even though my eyes are beginning to water.

"I get it," I say.

"I'm sorry," he says. He stands up and collects his things.

"Can I still come to your presentation?" I ask. "To support you."

"I won't stop you," he says, putting on his bag. "But you don't need to."

My chest squeezes at that. It hurts that he isn't asking me to be there. That he doesn't even care if I show up.

He pauses for a beat to look at me, then makes his way to the door. "I'll see you around, Dominic," he says.

I wait until he's at the door. "See you around," I say. And when the door clicks shut, I let the tears flow. I lay back into bed and let myself feel real sorry. I think I deserve this.

I came on this trip to find some worthwhile project to fund. I was hoping this would land me a woman. I just wanted to live a normal, straight life. Until Aaron Watkins, the man who took my virginity, walks right into my back and just so happens to be sharing a room with me. That has only one bed.

And then I remember how much I still care about the man. And he feels the same about me. We get dinner, reminisce. We got back to the hotel and have the most electrifying sex of my life. And what do I do the next day? I push him like the goddamn dickhead I am.

I sob into the duvet. Man, I've cursed a lot on this trip. But I swear none of the curses have been superfluous. I've needed each one. Life would have been so much easier if I just didn't go on this trip. If I really wanted, I could have used some other way to find a worthwhile cancer project to fund, or an easier way to attract a woman. That would have saved me a lot of heartache.

That's when it hits me. My crying ceases, and I sit up and stare at my puffy face in the dresser mirror.

That's it. I came on this whole trip to find a worthwhile project to fund, right? What if that's still what I'm meant to do?

Aaron researches leukemia in children. His presentation is later today, and he still needs funding. He said he's afraid that I'll find another reason to walk away from him again. And I don't blame him. I would think the same.

But what if I gave him a definitive reason to believe I would never do that again?

I shoot up from the bed, wipe my eyes, and take my phone out of my pocket, charged up by my excitement from this idea. I need to make some important calls—namely, to my lawyer and accountant. If I'm about to do what I'm about to do, I need to run it by them first.

But as my put my phone to my ear, I get the feeling that it will all work out the way it needs to.

So long as Aaron gives me one last chance.

Chapter 15

Aaron Watkins

As I watch my conference room fill up, my heart's beating so fast it's threatening to break my chest open. There are so many more people here than I expected to come on the last day of the conference. But I can't complain. All the more people to potentially fund me.

And I hate to admit it, but I'm also secretly wishing to find Dominic sitting somewhere in the audience.

After he came to apologize, I was relieved. I wanted to speak to him again. But after talking it all out, I realized that in getting back together with him, there was just going to be a repeat of what already happened. There was no way to guarantee that he wouldn't just run away when another opportunity arose, and I couldn't live with that. Winning my parents' love may no longer be my motivation in my career, but the fear that someone will leave me like they did still lingers. I'm just trying to look out for myself.

Then, it's time to begin. I step up to my podium. I scan the crowd, automatically searching for Dominic, but there are so many people here that I get lost in the sea of faces. Which is good. More people is better for me. Besides, Dominic definitely isn't here. I turned him down. I doubt he'd want to come after that.

As I start my presentation, my ears ring so loud I can't even perceive my own voice. But I buffed up my presentation and went over it so much this morning that I could practically do this in my sleep. So I just go on, pretending I'm calm and collected.

I talk about the field of leukemia research, what's been researched well and where the gaps are. The audience nods along, and some even scribble down notes as I speak. From what I can tell, there's a pretty good balance of academics and investors, which is flattering. Not only am I garnering the interest of people willing to fund me, but I'm also intriguing colleagues in the field. Take that, Bill. Maybe others really do find my work promising.

Speaking of promising, I finally reach the section where I talk about the implications of my own research. Which, after meeting with Bill, I heavily revised. Not to tone down my research or anything like that, but to assert the claim that my findings on this project could very well lead to the cure for leukemia.

When I make the bold claim, I'm practically sweating through my suit. I mostly look up at my slides during this section, afraid that many in the audience are scowling at my assertions. After all, Bill so far has been the only one to see this kind of potential in my research. Others might not see it like he or I do.

But when I glance down at the audience, I almost stop speaking. Because people are leaning forward in their chairs, listening in rapt curiosity and fascination. Several people lean over to the person next to them to whisper something, but their eyes remain fixed on me and my slides, as if what they are hearing is the most groundbreaking thing to hit the field of leukemia in decades. And I think they just might be.

"And before we go into the Q&A," I say, reaching the final part of my presentation. My voice begins to shake, and I have to take a deep breath to keep it still. "I want to share a little story about why I embarked on this journey so long ago." I take the microphone off the podium and walk to center stage, leaving me open and vulnerable.

After I finished buffing up my presentation this morning. There was something missing. Something personal to give it that punch. Plus, reflecting on my conversation with Bill, I didn't just want to say that I would offer my cure to the public for free. I wanted to provide an explanation why. And sharing the story about my sister and my family was the only way to do it. I've only gone into depth about this story with a few other people, including Dominic back at Miss U. I've never done it in front of this many people, let alone strangers. But if I really want to get funding with no strings attached, then this is what I have to do.

"When my sister was just five years old," I begin. "She was diagnosed with acute lymphocytic leukemia. And her prognosis did not look good. I was only eleven, but I remember watching the light leave her eyes as it dawned on her that she would not live a full life. Though she preserved her positive attitude, her disposition only became more somber as she grew."

The audience listens attentively, and I swear I could hear a pin drop in that large room. My eyes are heating up with tears, but I hold them back. I can do this. Just a little longer.

"But just before the illness took her life at eight years old, I sat at the side of her hospital bed with my mom and dad. She asked us, because she wasn't going to live her life, to live a happy life for her. And we all agreed."

The audience audibly 'awhs' at that, which only makes it more difficult to keep the tears at bay. This moment was one of the most traumatic of my life—watching her accept her imminent death. And that promise of happiness—my parents abandoned it only years after her death, while I sought to make it right by ending the suffering of others with leukemia. At least I was keeping that promise.

"After she died, I tried to keep that promise—to be happy. But that was harder for my parents. We never had a lot of money to begin with, so the compounding medical bills only drove our family further apart until finally both of them just died inside. They became husks of themselves, mourning their daughter and the life they could have lived with the money they lost. Growing up with parents like these only exacerbated the trauma of losing my sister."

Before I continue on with the rest of my story—explaining how I siphoned this trauma into desire to help those suffering from leukemia and how we shouldn't make them suffer more by jacking up the price of their cure—a large man stands up and shimmies to the walkway. And behind him is revealed the NFO player I was least expecting to see.

Dominic Johnson.

He's been here the whole time.

He offers a warm smile, and even this far away it makes my knees weak. I pause my story and brace myself against the podium.

The memory of my sister asking us to live a happy life completely takes over my mind. It's been so long since I've relived this memory, and retelling it to such an important audience has me thinking about it in new ways.

But why is Dominic's face making me relive it so vividly? It's remarkably clear now.

Because, just like my parents, I failed my sister's promise, too.

She asked me to be happy for her. Not others suffering from leukemia or their families. But me. Myself.

Yet I was miserable for years, letting myself believe that the only way I could ever deserve not to be miserable was to undo the hurt that transpired after my sister's diagnosis. But I could never do that. So I set out to save others from this hurt. In other words, I came to believe I was unworthy of happiness unless everyone else around me was happy first.

Why is this so clear now? Because Dominic is the one of the people that make me happiest. And I've continually pushed him away.

In college, I ran away from him before he was even drafted, afraid that the NFO would inevitably tear us apart. After I kissed him at this conference, I pushed him away again, saying that he couldn't be with me now that he was in the NFO or that I didn't have the time for a relationship. And even after he comes back to me and genuinely apologizes for what he did, asking to get back together, I push him away again, saying I just need to protect myself. All this because I was afraid of what could have happened if we dated.

But what if this wasn't what I was actually afraid of? What if, in reality, I was afraid that Dominic and I could work out? That we could have a loving relationship? That I could finally get the love and happiness I didn't think I deserved?

Laura rushes up to the edge of the stage. "Are you okay?" she mouths.

I nod to her, tears now streaming down my face. This thing about deserving and chasing after happiness was what Laura was trying to tell me in the restaurant yesterday. If I deprioritize my own happiness, then I'll never be satisfied. Just like Angelica Schuyler.

"Sorry," I say, my lips quivering into the microphone. I wipe my eyes. "Just—it's—wow. You know that feeling when you just realize something life changing that you never saw before?"

Many in the audience nod.

"Yeah, you know what I mean," I say. I glance at Dominic, and he's leaned forward onto his knees, his brow furrowed and jaw locked, listening intently. I think he may even be crying too. So I decide to stand up straighter and finish my story. I'm doing this for myself, but I know he'd want me to finish it, too.

"And so," I continue. "I blamed myself. Like traumatized children tend to do, I blamed myself for my sister's death and my parent's estrangement. I told myself I couldn't be happy until everyone else suffering from leukemia was. And it wasn't until just now that I realized how insidiously deep this belief dug itself inside me. It wasn't until a man I very much love helped me see that."

Dominic lifts a fist to his heart and smiles, tears streaming down his face too. Around him several others are crying, and I feel galvanized to end with my final point.

"There is so much suffering that comes with this illness," I say. "And not just from the leukemia itself, but from the cost of the treatment and trauma of grief. So if any of you are professionally interested in working with me, that's what you need to understand above all else—that we're not just working to end a disease. We're working to end the rippling trauma that comes with disease and the loss of life." I pause and take a deep breath. "And that means that if and when my treatment leads to a cure, there will be no patent. The cure to leukemia will be free to the public."

There's a mixed reaction in the audience. Some clap and cheer, while others audibly scoff and complain. There are even several people who stand out and walk out after that. But Dominic's sitting back in his chair, his arms folded, and he's smiling at me like I personally distributed the cure to leukemia to the public myself.

"Thank you for coming to my presentation," I say. "I'm happy to answer any questions." And when I set the microphone back in its socket, the room goes wild.

I step down to the table next to the stage to answer questions, and Laura immediately comes to my side.

"That was amazing," she says, squeezing my arm. But we don't have long to talk before I'm swarmed. Several other researchers come up to ask me questions, and then, to my relief, some investors. But they don't express immediate interest. They try to get me to walk back on my desire to not patent the cure, but I don't budge. And so they don't ask to meet with me further or to even get my contact information.

"It's gonna be okay," Laura says as I bite my nails. "There are still plenty of people in here. We'll find someone."

"Should I have even announced that?" I ask, referring to my story and my desire to not patent the cure. "Now no one's gonna—"

"Stop it," she says, turning to me. "You followed your conscience, and that is beautiful. There are few people in history who are as noble as you to do what you've done. Just like Emmett from *Legally Blonde*, you had your chip on your shoulder. You were traumatized as a child by the loss of your sister and your parents who drifted away from you. But instead of using this to justify a desire for riches, you chose to be selfless and give the future cure to leukemia away for free so no one would have to endure what you did. That's brave. That's honest. That's kind. That's you."

Tears come to my eyes. "Your musical allusions continue to impress me."

"Well, sooner or later we'll have a musical out about the man who cured leukemia!"

I hug her and plant a kiss on her cheek. "Thank you," I say.

As we wait for folks to come talk to me, I think back on what Dominic said just days before. He, too, said I was kind for selflessly trying to help others instead of wallowing in the pain. I just wish that I loved myself enough to allow myself happiness and let Dominic back into my life while I had the chance. I hope he's still here. I'd love to talk to him if he still wants me.

Pretty soon, everyone's filtering out of the room, and I have to remind myself that I had them all at the edge of their seats at one point. Because they sure don't seem to give a shit about me now. I don't see Dominic, so I figure he's gone, too. So much for making up with him.

A woman in elegant clothing only a rich Brooklynite would wear approaches the table. "Absolutely touching story," she says. "But you really ought to rethink the patent thing. Nobody will ever fund you if they get nothing in return."

And I'm tempted to flip her off as she strolls out the door, but I keep it together. But Laura doesn't hold back.

I lower her arm. "Hey, I don't want to antagonize anyone here further."

"Sorry," she says, putting her hand on her pregnant belly. "I'm just pissed."

I fold my arms and sigh. "Me too."

When the room's empty, the conference all but over, I lean forward onto the table and bury my face in my arms. Laura rubs my back, and I'm so worn out from the last hour that I think I could sleep for at least three days.

"Welp, back to Iowa," I say into my arms. "And my last year as a professor. Because Iowa's definitely not going to keep me on without funding."

Laura stops rubbing and doesn't respond, which is definitely not like her.

"What's wrong?" I ask, my face still in my arms. When she still doesn't respond, I'm about to raise my head, but that's when there's a loud thud on the table. My head shoots up, and I see the beautiful Dominic Johnson standing in front of our table, a thick stack of papers right in between us. And they're hot.

"Dominic," I say. "What are you—"

"This isn't the final contract, obviously, but I wanted to provide a mockup. Our lawyers would have to go over specifics, but the bare bones are in here. I had to beg, and pay, hotel staff to print it out for me, which is why I'm showing up now," he says, almost out of breath. "And careful—the paper's still hot."

I look up at the strawberry blonde hunk like he's the sun blinding me. "What the hell are you talking about?"

"I'm in," he says. "I want to fund your project."

Chapter 16

Dominic Johnson

AARON STARES UP AT me like I've just spoken a forgotten language, and my heart is beating faster than it has in the few playoff games I've reached. I've just offered to fund Aaron's project. There's logistics to iron out, sure, but I know his demands are within my NFO salary budget. And his project is definitely worth every penny. He said it, and I believe it. I think the man I love may have discovered the cure to leukemia. And this time, I'm choosing to fund the project because of what it can do and the man behind it—and maybe for one other personal reason. But this reason isn't to find some woman. It's one I think Aaron might like.

The woman sitting next to Aaron has her mouth hung open, then covers it like she done something horribly improper. She glares at Aaron as if doting him on to speak. But he's dead silent.

"You said you were afraid I'd find some other reason to leave you," I say, bringing up my third reason I'm offering to fund him. "But this contract right here is a commitment. A promise. One that says I won't just walk away from you."

He thumbs through the papers and shakes his head with his jaw dropped.

"Of course," I say. "If we got back together but you wanted to leave me in the future, we'd work it out. I'm not shackling me to you. But I'd obviously still fund your project regardless. I just miss you. I want to be with you again. If you'll have me."

Aaron stands up and walks around the table. He stands right in front of me, and my stomach sinks to the ground. He props himself up on the stack of papers that will make up our contract, puts his hand on his hip and looks up at me curiously.

My heart races like crazy. I need to know what he's thinking. Does he want me back or not?

"If you need some time to think about it," I say. "I'm happy to—"

And then he plants his lips on mine. His sweet taste intoxicates me, and I breathe in his earthy, masculine scent. My tongue searches his mouth, and I wrap my arms around his back. More than anything, I want to tear his clothes apart right now. And I could cry with how happy I am to have him back in my arms. The dark storms of my mind have parted, and the sun is shining bright. There's no one else I could possibly want.

He pulls away and looks me in the eyes. "Yeah, we have some details to iron out," I say. "But I say yes to a partnership. In both senses of the term."

I smile and kiss him again, unable to contain myself. "My feelings for you aside, I think you're the project I would have chosen."

He scoffs. "You're just saying that."

"Aaron Watkins, are you still going to put yourself down after all you said up there?"

He blushes, and I swear I hear his lady friend swoon behind me.

"Well thank you," he says, still blushing. And it makes his handsome face look all the better.

"It's brilliant," I say. "And kind. Offering up your cure for free? You're a legend, Aaron. A legend."

He starts crying again, and I reach out to catch the falling fear with my thumb. Then I plant a gentle kiss right above his eye. I pull him tight into me, then rub his back, wishing that I could be doing this skin to skin.

"You two should get a room," the woman says, collecting her things. When she stands up, I try not to gawk at how pregnant she is.

"We do have a room," Aaron says with a laugh.

The woman extends her hand to me. "Laura."

"Dominic," I say, shaking hers.

"So you're the NFO player who stole my best friends' heart."

"And I'm hoping I can keep it," I say, grinning at Aaron.

She smiles at Aaron. "I like him. Especially after all that he just did. He's a keeper."

Aaron looks up at me, absolutely beaming. "Thank you," he says. "For coming. For offering to fund me. For asking for me back."

I look back at him like he's the only person in this world. Because, considering all that matters right now, he really is.

"We really should go back to our room," he says.

"You think?" Laura says. "I can practically feel the hormones and testosterone coming off the both of you. It's the last night of the conference. Go blow off some steam."

I extend my elbow to Aaron, and he puts his arm through it. I pick up our contract, and we turn toward the door.

"Ready?" I ask.

He leans his head against me, then kisses my shoulder. "Ready."

We wish Laura a goodbye and head to the elevators. The lobby is busy with academics and investors alike rushing to make their flights. But suddenly, Aaron lets go of my arm, and we both freeze.

"What?" I ask, my heart racing again.

"You're in the NFO," he says. "You can't be seen with me. They'd—I don't know, kick you out?"

I grab his hand like I mean it. "Walk with me," I say with a tilt of my head. "And don't let go."

And he obeys just like he does in bed.

"Nobody here recognizes me," I say. "I'm nothing famous like Kyle Weaver is. So I don't have to worry about getting caught."

We reach the elevator and press the button. Once the doors open, I usher inside the empty elevator. And when those doors close, I pick Aaron up even with the contract in my hand. His legs wrap around me, and I press him against the wall as our tongues dance together.

When the elevator dings, I drop him, and we brush ourselves off as we step onto the sixth floor. Luckily, no one is around to see what a mess we are.

"I gave this some thought this morning before I printed up the contract," I say, holding his hand as we walk to our room. "I'm not ashamed of you, Aaron. If I could, I'd tell the whole world tonight that you're my man and that I'm proud of it. I mean, I love football, but you're more important. Fuck what the NFO thinks."

He gasps at my swear, but I say the word to show him I mean business.

"But if I'm to fund your project, at least for the next few years," I say, keeping my voice low. "I need to stay playing and making money. And if they found out I was openly gay, I'm sure management would find a way to oust me."

We reach our door, and I put my free hand on his shoulder as I face him. "I believe in your project, Aaron. I really do. I'm willing to keep our relationship under wraps at least until I retire or another donor comes along. And since I play in St. Louis and you're at Admiral University in Iowa, we'd also have to do long distance. Not ideal, I know, but I'd plan on visiting as much as possible and moving up there once I retire. Because you're worth it.

"But I can't make this decision for you. If you'd rather not keep it a secret, we can figure things out. If you'd rather end the whole relationship now—" I sigh, unable to fathom such a thing. "—I'll let it happen for you. So the decision is yours. I'll go with what you decide."

He opens his mouth, but before he can reply, I scan our key card and let us into our room so we have full privacy. I place the contract down on the dresser and lean against it as he sits on the edge of the bed, chewing his lips in thought.

Then he looks up at me, his decision made. He gets off the bed and comes to me, he presses his body against mine, and my rod is already getting hard. He starts untying my tie, watching me as he does.

"I want you," he says. And my heart leaps with joy.

"And I also want us to be out and authentic," he continues. "But I don't want that to get in the way of what might be the biggest cure of the 21st century so far."

"Me too," I say, watching his lips.

"So I say we stay a secret," he says. "And do long distance. Only as long as we absolutely have to."

Relieved, I grab the sides of his head and give him my biggest kiss yet. "Good," I say, pulling away. "Because I couldn't imagine a life without you."

He starts unbuttoning my shirt, and I slide off his suit coat as I kiss him, revealing his broad shoulders. Pretty soon, we're shirtless, then naked.

"I never had sex with Jenna, by the way," I say. "Just thought you should know."

He kisses me. "Good. Now enough talk. Because I want you to fuck me until I can't walk."

I chuckle, already rock-hard. "And then I might let you cum."

He moans and bites my lip, and I groan with pleasure.

"Ruin me, Dominic Johnson," he says into my ear. "I can take it."

And that's all the invitation I need.

I push him back onto the bed, his manly body on full display. And before he can move, I put myself between his legs and pin his arms down. I reach over to the nightstand lamp to turn out the lights, so all we have is the natural summer light pouring in from outside. I take out the lube I left in the drawer here and squirt some onto my hands. Aaron's got his hands under his knees, pulling his legs back and presenting his hairy hole to me.

"Hope you don't mind that we get right to it," I say, coating my shaft with lube.

"All the more dick for—ahh."

I shut him up when I put my lubed finger inside him, stroking myself to stay as hard as possible. And once I can't wait any longer, I insert myself inside the man I love.

"Oh, fuck," Aaron says once I'm fully inside him. "I've missed you so much."

I nod. "Good. I know you have. Keep buttering me up."

"Please, God," he groans. "I just want to please you. I want you to use me."

I pause. "Les Mis—just making sure that's what you really want to do?"

He nods. "I'm your cumslut. I'm so mad at myself for holding myself back from you for all these years. If I didn't jerk off to thought of you every day, then that was a good week. Because I couldn't keep you out of my mind."

I can't help but smirk.

"God, that face," he says. "For so long, I haven't let myself be happy. Even in the bedroom. And tonight, that changes."

"Alright," I say, leaning forward, still hard as ever inside him. "I want you to be happy, too. Tell me what I can do."

"Use me, like I said. Fuck me. Cum inside me. God, please, more than once if you can. Make me edge the whole time. Then, once you've absolutely used me up, when you're dog tired, put that gorgeous man cock in my mouth and let me nurse it until I can't hold it anymore. I don't even care that I haven't douched. Just wash it off and let me have it. I need to worship your sexy body with my mouth."

"Christ," I say, not even ashamed to take his name in vain. Because Aaron'll get me to cum from his desperate words alone.

But then I squint at him, puzzled. "I can do all that," I say. "But you said yourself you've been holding off your own happiness. Isn't edging doing exactly that?"

He shakes his head and squeezes his hole around my penis, making my breath quicken. "Not at all," he says. "Because I get the pleasure of having a man get off inside me. I get the pleasure of having my hole pounded over and over again. Holding myself just before the point of relief enhances the pleasure of all this exponentially, and when I finally do release, it's like a one-way ticket to heaven. Trust me. I know what I'm doing now. I just really, really need you and only you to fuck me like you really fucking mean it."

"Goddamn," I say. "Alright. You don't have to tell me twice."

And then I start pounding him like a bull ready to breed, commanding him to stroke himself slowly but steadily. I dig my hands into his shoulders, gripping him hard as I thrust into him. But then I get worried I'll bruise him, so I loosen my grip. And that's when he shakes his head and gets me to squeeze just as hard as I was. And this whole deal gets me to cum in less than ten minutes, especially considering this is only the second time we've had sex in seven years, and this is the first time that neither of us are holding back.

"You keep that dick inside me," he says, almost feral. "I need it like I need to fucking breathe."

And that accelerates my grace period. I'm hard again, faster than I would expect.

"And you keep stroking yourself," I say. "Faster this time, you hear me?"

He nods. "Anything, Dominic," he says, picking up the pace.

"On your knees," I say.

We get in position to do doggy, but it isn't enough. I want to see more of him—as much of his body as I can. This is my boyfriend, for Pete's sake. My fucking boyfriend. I'm letting myself finally say that to myself. And I want to see all of him for the man that he is.

"Put your hands on the headboard," I say, not fully understanding what I'm trying to do but knowing, in my bones, it's what we need to do. "Only one hand, though. That other one better be stroking."

He obeys, moving his body quickly and confidently, showing that he doesn't feel as self-conscious as he did the first night we had sex. Which is good, because there's no reason for him to feel self-conscious with how good he looks, especially in this position—his huge, hairy back on full display.

"Spread your legs," I growl, going feral for his huge, perfect body. And he does, showing off those thick, hairy thighs.

"Now poke your butt out."

And Christ Almighty, when he does I swear I'm already about to cum a second time. His butt cheeks are bigger than the planet we stand on, and his hairy hole is practically begging for more. I stick my hard manhood in him again, and he moans and bucks back on it.

"Oh yeah," I say. "Exactly like that." I watch as he bounces up and down on my rod, his back, thighs, and butt all flexed for me and only me. To think that I would have given this up to live a life with some woman? I'm sure there are men who look at women like I do Aaron right now. But good for them. Because that's definitely not me.

I grab his cheeks and thrust inside him hungrily, feeling the heat of another orgasm come onto me already. And then I let out a guttural groan as I release my second load inside him tonight.

"God, that's good," he says, still in this sexy position.

I wipe sweat from my forehead as I pull out of him. "I'm not done with you yet."

"Thank God."

He turns around and faces me, and I let him give his shaft a break. I then pull him in for a kiss, and we hold each other there for one moment or ten. I lose count.

I pull away, then look into those brown eyes. "I love you so fucking much, Aaron Watkins," I say, using the f-word because I mean it. "I'm glad you took me back."

He brushes my cheek with his thumb, and for a moment, I'm afraid he won't reciprocate—that any moment he'll change his mind and decide to push me away again.

"I love you, too, Dominic Johnson," he says, then plants a soft kiss on my chin, dismissing the last of my fears. "I'm looking forward to a life together."

That's when he lowers himself, wipes me off with a nearby towel, and gets to sucking.

"This is how I want the third," he says, my length semi-hard in his mouth.

"Gonna take me a while," I say.

"Good," he says, stroking the underside of my penis with his tongue. "Let me work for it."

"Good boy," I say. "And your break is over."

He flips onto his back, puts my manhood in his mouth, and gets to masturbating again.

"You cum when I say," I remind him. "And be sure to say my name. Even with your mouth full."

He nods, my length still in his mouth. It's already getting hard again. Dang, Aaron Watkins is good.

I'll be honest: I had my doubts that Aaron would get me off a third time. But pretty soon I find myself over him, my butt on his chest, thrusting my rock-hard shaft into his mouth. When he makes choking, gargled noises, I stop, but then he gets upset and makes me start up again. Man, my boyfriend's insatiable. And I love it.

I have one of his arms pinned back, his other one stroking his manhood. His legs writhe, and he moans like his entire body has been dipped in some pleasure goo. He was right. Edging this much really does make him feel good.

"Don't get too greedy," I say. "It's me first."

He nods and sucks me more enthusiastically. As I watch his beautiful face contort in pleasure while he sucks my length like it's going to save his life, I feel the heat of my climax reach me again. I knew I never should have doubted Aaron's abilities. Because I'm about to get off a third time, and that's a record for me.

"Oh, Aaron," I grunt as I empty my seed inside him, and he moans in ecstasy as he sucks me even harder. I hear him slurping me up, making sure he has every last drop. Then, he looks up, my rod still hard in his mouth. I'm dog-tired, just as he said I would be, so it's time I let him have it.

"I think you've earned it," I say. "Be a good boy and cum for me."

He swallows my length as deep as he can, then strokes his length fast. His tongue massages my manhood like it's his personal pacifier, and his nose is pressed so deep into my crotch I wouldn't think he was breathing if I couldn't feel it.

He moans loudly, and I know it's time.

"Dominic," he says, gargled with my rod in his mouth. He shoots so explosively that some of it thwacks against my butt. I look back, and a clear line of white goodness trails up from his penis right to my cheeks.

"Oh man, Dominic," he says, releasing my shaft. "That was—I don't—"

I lean down to kiss him, his body still convulsing from his orgasm. When I pull away, he looks at me like the angel Peter at the gates of heaven. He opens his mouth, but nothing comes out. I chuckle. I've made him speechless.

I take the nearby towel and wipe us both off. Then I pull him under the covers and hold him tight just like I did on the first night. Except this time, I can finally call him mine again.

"My flight's not until tonight," I whisper into his ear. "We got time to relax."

He holds my arms and nuzzles into me, and God does he fit perfectly.

"I just want to lay here with you," he says. "If I haven't worn you out, maybe a round two. Or round four in your case."

I laugh and squeeze him, planting a kiss on the back of the neck. I breathe in his scent and swear I'll never be sad again.

"Or we can go to dinner," he says. "I don't care. So long as it's with my boyfriend who makes me happy."

Boyfriend.

Before going on this trip, I never would have thought to reconnect with the man who stole my virginity and my heart. But I'm so glad I did. Because if not, I could have been off with some girl I don't love by now. And boy am I glad I didn't do that. I'm happy that I'm finally picking someone I really love and being true to myself.

I squeeze him one last time, feeling sleep come on. "As long as I'm holding you," I say, yawning. "I'm set for life."

Epilogue—One Year Later

Aaron Watkins

As Dominic and I walk into the dimly lit Broadway theatre, he sneakily reaches out to hold my hand.

I whip my head to him. "What if someone sees?" I hiss. But I don't let go. "You still have at least another two years in the NFO."

He squeezes my hand and leans into me as we walk down to our seats. "It's dark in here," he says. "And besides, I'm gonna take any opportunity I can to show you how much I love you." Then he kisses the side of my head.

"Dominic!" I say as if he just dropped the f-bomb.

He manages to kiss me on the cheek one more time before I bat him away. And that's when I see Laura and Patrick waving at us. We quickly shimmy past the few folks sitting down and get in our seats next to them.

Laura greets the both of us by squeezing our hands, and this is the first time I've seen her baby bump gone in person.

"How is it without Elizabeth?" I ask, referring to her daughter named after Patrick's mother. And the other Schuyler sister.

Laura sighs, and Patrick holds her hand.

"It's not easy," Patrick says.

"She's my little boo bear, and I miss her."

"The nanny's taking good care of her," Patrick says, rubbing her hand.

"I know," she says, nodding. "But this is good. We needed a break." She turns to Dominic. "Thanks for inviting us."

"My pleasure," my boyfriend says. "I finally get to see *The Book of Mormon* on Broadway."

I squeeze his knee. "You're going to love it."

The four of us catch up with each other while we wait for the show to begin. It's been a whirlwind of a year, but an amazing one nonetheless. Once the school year began, Dominic's funding kicked in. By then, I had managed to cobble together a research team to put in the first stages of my plan to create a new form of chemotherapy—the one that Bill, the very first investor I met, said could lead to the cure in leukemia. And by the end of the academic year, we were already seeing results in our trial groups, results that have been attracting the attention of the most prominent academics and wealthiest investors in the field, many of whom laud me for not wanting to patent the cure to leukemia. Dominic and I are hoping that, by this time next year, I'll have more diverse funds, putting less pressure on him to fund me entirely.

But my relationship with Dominic couldn't be better. It's not ideal that I live in Iowa and he in St. Louis, but any time that he isn't practicing or playing, he's with me, and I use any time I have to see him. Once   we've found funding to replace Dominic, he can quietly retire from the NFO and come live with me. And then we can be out and open about our love. He and I can't wait for that date.

Soon, the musical begins, and I'm already beaming. This is one of my favorites, but I've never seen it on Broadway, and Dominic hasn't seen it at all. This is going to be fabulous.

Even ten minutes into the show, Dominic has a smile just as wide as mine. I love seeing him this happy. He's mentioned to me how he thought what he needed was to be with a woman because it was the normal, less shameful thing to do. But he felt so miserable doing it, like there was a storm cloud perpetually raining down on his mind. And when we got back together, he said I was the opposite, like a ray of sunshine warming his skin or a body of water cooling him down on a hot day. And I have to admit that he feels the exact same to me.

Sometimes, my fears stemming from childhood have reared their ugly heads, making me think that I don't deserve a relationship this nice. And when it gets really bad, it feels like there's a little devil on my shoulder telling me to sabotage it all—my relationship, my career, my life. Just like I did with Dominic multiple times now.

But in working with my therapist, I've learned that these feelings come and go, and I don't have to let them control me. Besides, I know my worth now, and I know that I'm deserving of happiness just like everyone else. And most importantly that I don't need to make others happy before I tend to my own needs and desires. This has made both loving and being loved by Dominic rigorous, all-encompassing, ennobling, and euphoric down to a tee.

When we get to "Turn It Off", the song about flipping the light switch of sexuality, Dominic grins, grabs my hand, and leans over to me.

"I was a fool to ever think I could have turned my gayness," he says. "Especially for you."

Not seeing any other legitimate option, I kiss him right there and hold it like we're the only ones in the whole theatre. His hand caresses the back of my neck, and then I pull away, happier than I've ever been.

"I love you, Dominic," I say.

"Love you, too, Aaron."

And then we watch the rest of the show, holding hands and beaming. Not just because we're entertained but because we've finally let ourselves love each other again.

What's Next?

Enjoyed Downing Dominic? Check out *Catching Kyle*, book one in the Football Heartthrobs series, now!